The Yalta Incident

By

Patrick Mitchell

Best Wishes

Patrick Mitchell

2QT Limited (Publishing)

First edition 2022 by 2QT Limited (Publishing)
Settle, North Yorkshire BD24 9BZ

Cover design Charlotte Mouncey
Cover image created with images from Brandon Hoogenboom and Caleb George on Unsplash.com maps and flags from Istockphoto.comy

Publisher disclaimer

This story is both based and inspired by a true story so whilst some events and place names are real, they are described according to the authors' recollection; recognition and understanding of the events. Characters in this book other than those clearly in the public domain, have either been changed to protect their annonimity or are fictitious. As such the Publisher does not hold any responsibility for any inaccuracies or opinions expressed by the author.

Printed in Great Britain by IngramSparks UK
A CIP catalogue record for this book is available
from the British Library
ISBN 978-1-914083-53-2

This book is dedicated to my darling wife, Margaret,
whose encouragement and support
during very difficult times, has been invaluable.

Prologue

Special Message to the Congress on Urgent National Needs President John F. Kennedy

Delivered in person before a joint session of Congress May 25, 1961 Excerpt of Section IX: Space

... Finally, if we are to win the battle that is now going on around the world between freedom and tyranny, the dramatic achievements in space which occurred in recent weeks should have made clear to us all, as did the Sputnik in 1957, the impact of this adventure on the minds of men everywhere, who are attempting to make a determination of which road they should take. Since early in my term, our efforts in space have been under review. With the advice of the Vice President, who is Chairman of the National Space Council, we have examined where we are strong and where we are not, where we may succeed and where we may not. Now it is time to take longer strides--time for a great new American enterprise--time for this nation to take a clearly leading role in space achievement, which in many ways may hold the key to our future on earth.

I believe we possess all the resources and talents necessary. But the facts of the matter are that we have never made the national decisions or marshaled the national resources required for such leadership. We have never specified long-range goals on an urgent time schedule, or managed our resources and our time so as to insure their fulfillment.

Recognizing the head start obtained by the Soviets with their large rocket engines, which gives them many months of lead-time, and recognizing the likelihood that they will exploit this lead for some time to come in still more impressive successes, we nevertheless are required to make new efforts on our own. For while we cannot guarantee that we shall one day be first, we can guarantee that any failure to make this effort will make us last. We take an additional risk by making it in full view of the world, but as shown by the feat of astronaut Shepard, this very risk enhances our stature when we are successful. But this is not merely a race. Space is open to us now; and our eagerness to share its meaning is not governed by the efforts of others. We go into space because whatever mankind must undertake, free men must fully share.

I therefore ask the Congress, above and beyond the increases I have earlier requested for space activities, to provide the funds which are needed to meet the following national goals:

First, I believe that this nation should commit itself to achieving the goal, before this decade is out, of landing a man on the moon and returning him safely to the earth. No single space project in this period will be more impressive to mankind, or more important for the long-range exploration of space; and none will be so difficult or expensive to accomplish. We propose to accelerate the development of the appropriate lunar space craft. We propose to develop alternate liquid and solid fuel boosters, much larger than any now being developed, until certain which is superior. We propose additional funds for other engine development and for unmanned explorations--explorations which are particularly important for one purpose which this nation will never overlook: the survival of the man who first makes this daring flight. But in a very real sense, it will not be one man going to the moon--if we make this judgment affirmatively, it will be an entire nation. For all of us must work to put him there.

...I believe we should go to the moon. But I think every citizen of this country as well as the Members of the Congress should consider the matter carefully in making their judgment, to which we have given attention over many weeks and months, because it is a heavy burden, and there is no sense in agreeing or desiring that the United States take an affirmative position in outer space, unless we are prepared to do the work and bear the burdens to make it successful. If we are not, we should decide today and this year.

This decision demands a major national commitment of scientific and technical manpower, materiel and facilities, and the possibility of their diversion from other important activities where they are already thinly spread. It means a degree of dedication, organization and discipline which have not always characterized our research and development efforts. It means we cannot afford undue work stoppages, inflated costs of material or talent, wasteful interagency rivalries, or a high turnover of key personnel.

1

A Problem

The chief of MI6, Sir Richard Temple, was in a pensive mood as he left Number 10 Downing Street and made his way to his office in Birdcage Walk. He walked through St James's Park, not in his customary brisk style, but slowly, deep in thought after his weekly meeting with the prime minister. He did not hear the quacking of the ducks nor the roar of the traffic down The Mall. He was preoccupied with one of the most intriguing and important problems of his career.

Usually, his Tuesday appointment with the prime minister was over within half an hour. His briefing papers had been sent on the day before. He would then answer any queries raised during the meeting, give the latest intelligence reports on the major projects, enjoy an excellent cup of Brazilian coffee and some light-hearted political gossip with his master, then leave.

But today had been very different. When he entered the prime minister's private study, he had been surprised to find another person present. This was most unusual. Even the prime minister's personal secretary was not allowed to stay in the room when he met with the head of British Intelligence.

'Good morning, Sir Richard,' said the prime minister as

he extended his hand to greet him. 'Let me introduce you to Strobe Delaney, the American ambassador. I am afraid we have a problem.'

Sir Richard shook the big, warm hand of the tall Texan, who he had met once before about five years earlier while he had been working with the CIA in Washington during the Cuban missile crisis in 1962. Delaney had that rare gift of having been trusted by the charismatic President Kennedy and his successor, President Johnson. Kennedy had soon recognised his potential and had quickly promoted him to be his chief presidential advisor on external security, which entailed liaising with the CIA on highly classified material.

After the traumatic assassination of the president he was kept on by Johnson, who wished to ensure continuity of security policy but felt he could not trust many of the old Kennedy clan, who viewed the new president as a dull usurper of their former Camelot. The Texan Johnson knew he could rely on the Texan Delaney, and he was not disappointed.

With presidential patronage and his own exceptional qualities, Delaney's career took off. He held a succession of key posts in both the White House and the State Department until early in 1967 when he was appointed as the US ambassador to the Court of St James. The growing problem of Vietnam was producing unprecedented anti-American feeling among the populations of normally friendly countries. The president wanted his own man in London to keep an eye on Europe and to strengthen the special relationship with America's oldest ally.

The three men sat in comfortable chairs around a small low table, on which was placed a jug of piping hot coffee, three cups and saucers and a plate of light, thin biscuits. The prime minister poured out the coffee then turned to Sir Richard and said,

'The president has asked Mr Delaney to explain to me a major problem, which could have a profound effect on the credibility of the United States and its leadership of the Western Alliance. He has also asked for our help in resolving it. I thought it appropriate that the ambassador should also brief you on the details. Hence this meeting.'

During the next half hour Strobe Delaney outlined in his slow Texan drawl what had happened, what could happen, what was needed, and why British intelligence was vital in helping to resolve the problem. He explained that the United States had made good progress in developing their Moon project but had encountered major problems with rocket technology. The Soviets were ahead in this particular field, as their Soyuz space programme had demonstrated.

The ambassador confirmed that they had no agents behind the Iron Curtain, due to recent defections and captures. The president would welcome the help of the British government in obtaining through its espionage network any information it could on Soviet rockets. He spoke without interruption, stopping only occasionally to sip his coffee, and murmuring, 'Damn good coffee,' before continuing with his sombre explanations.

When he had finished, the prime minister and Sir Richard remained silent for a short while as if overcome with the enormity of it all. The prime minister then broke the silence and assured the ambassador that everything possible would be done to assist in this matter. He would personally speak to the president later that day. Delaney then stood up, thanked the prime minister, wished Sir Richard the best of luck, and was shown out by a Downing Street official who had been summoned to the room by telephone. The prime minister and the chief of security were then left alone.

'Well, Richard, this is going to be a hard nut to crack, particularly with the loss of so many of our agents in Soviet territory due to Blake's defection last year. If Dante is caught before mid September it will be an unmitigated disaster. This is our worst crisis since Khrushchev installed his nuclear missiles in Cuba. Do we have any agents in the field who are currently unknown to the Soviets?'

'No, Prime Minister.'

'How long does it take before an officer is ready for active duty?'

'At a minimum, between four to six months, but it usually takes at least a year before an officer is fully trained and operational, physically and psychologically.'

'You haven't got a year, or even four months. You have less than two. Failure is not an option. You have my complete authority to deal with this crisis as you think fit. However, I must agree your final plan before it is given the go-ahead. Please report back to me on Saturday morning with a coherent strategy.'

'Yes, sir, I'll do my best.'

By the time Sir Richard had arrived at Birdcage Walk, he knew he had to make two telephone calls. His personal executive assistant, Jennifer Ashworth, met him at his office door with an armful of files, all marked *Urgent* or *Important*. She was a little irritated by his late arrival, since she took pride in managing her boss through an exacting schedule.

'Put those files back in your office, Jennifer,' said Sir Richard, 'then get me the Foreign Secretary and the Home Secretary on the phone, Code Red.'

The top-secret red code told Jennifer she would have a long day – and night.

2

Tom Gillespie

The mild summer sea breeze blew in across Aberdeen Harbour, carrying with it the pungent smell of the morning's fish landings, which were by now long past their best. The auctions had taken place about three hours ago, and the discarded remnants were left to rot – much to the delight of the shrieking gulls.

The big Russian trawler was tied up by the quayside like a beached whale, gently swaying in the swell of the harbour. There was nobody on deck except a short, squat man with what looked like a long black sausage in his hand – which he occasionally bit into, chewed, then spat out towards the circling seagulls. He seemed to be enjoying himself, and grimaced a smile when a gull caught the titbit before it hit the ground.

'It won't be long before I visit his country,' Tom Gillespie, a junior officer in HM Customs and Excise, said to himself as he strolled round the harbour during his lunch break. The meeting with his boss, the controller of Customs and Excise, Scotland East, was at 2 p.m. Usually, such meetings did not take long: a general review of job performance followed by a routine warning about going to Communist countries, then a pint in the Copper Kettle pub if the boss had the time or the inclination.

However, Tom was not looking forward to this meeting. Robert Macalister was only recently appointed from London headquarters, and he had a reputation for discipline, insistence on the minutiae of departmental regulations and an abhorrence of any officer who, through lax conduct, brought the department into disrepute. Tom knew he was in for a rough ride.

The granite stone Custom House on Union Street was an imposing building: solid, dependable, built to last. It always struck Tom as comical that its inhabitants and fellow toilers in the wider regions of revenue control were lumped with the dregs of society, the riff-raff. Tax collectors have always been seen as a rum bunch: shifty, bureaucratic thieves who extort money from innocent victims.

He went to the second floor and entered the controller's outer office, which was occupied by his secretary, Morag Teesdale. She was a woman in her early forties who liked to think she was still only twenty-four. She wore expensive make-up, and in shaded light she still looked attractive. Her skirts were invariably very short to show off her fine legs, and in summer she wore light, sleeveless blouses with necklines which plunged, but not too far. Her full name was hardly ever used. She was universally known as Miss Tees.

'Hello, Tom,' she said. 'What have you been getting up to?' and gave him a knowing, flirtatious smile.

'Oh, nothing much, Morag,' Tom replied, looking her straight in the eyes and trying not to lower his own eyes to her chest.

'That's not what I've heard,' she said, and stepped out from behind her desk to reveal a white miniskirt with matching slingback high heels. 'Mr Macalister didn't seem very pleased when he went through your report this morning. Perhaps you might like a bit of company this evening to take your mind off a few things,' she said archly.

'I don't think my girlfriend would be too happy about that,' he said, which was a lie, since they had just split up. But he was sure that a few pints in the Blue Lamp with the lads would be preferable to a night of unrestrained passion with Miss Tees.

'The controller will now see you, Tom,' she said. 'Good luck,' and she opened the large oak door to reveal the stern-looking man behind an equally stern-looking mahogany desk.

'Come in, Gillespie. Sit down.'

Tom did as he was told.

3

The Meeting

Robert Macalister was dressed in a light grey suit, a white shirt and a blue silk Cambridge tie. His black hair was now flecked with grey, which correctly reflected his forty-six years. He looked the quintessential British civil servant – and was. His desk was completely clear, except for an onyx pen set and an open Manila file. His eyes slowly went from the file to an anxious Tom Gillespie.

'Since you arrived from London a year ago, your work and private life seems to have deteriorated, although there were already indications of a slide in your last report by the controller at London Central.'

He read slowly and deliberately from the file. '*A willing and intelligent officer, but he needs to show more commitment and responsibility to his work and to senior management. Reports of his private life show he is overly fond of alcohol, all-night parties, fast cars and fast women, particularly air stewardesses. He is regularly late for early morning rosters, and has been found asleep on at least two occasions in the restroom when he should have been on duty in the customs hall. He has been insubordinate to local managers, and after one such incident was disciplined and strictly monitored on restricted duties for two months.*'

Macalister paused and looked at Tom, obviously

expecting a comment. Tom remained silent, for he knew there was more to come. His eyes met the controllers for a second then turned downwards, sufficiently subdued.

There was a light tap on the door and Morag's face peered round.

'Shall I bring some coffee in now, Mr Macalister?'

Thank God for that, Tom thought. *A shot of caffeine would help me through the rest of this ordeal.*

'No, thank you, Morag,' said Macalister. 'We are not yet ready.'

Swine, Tom thought. *I bloody well am.* But he nodded in feigned agreement.

Macalister turned over a page in Tom's file and said somewhat sarcastically, 'I'm sure you would like to hear comments about your present performance and lifestyle, wouldn't you?'

'Oh, no, I wouldn't,' Tom said to himself. 'But I think I'm going to.'

The controller started to read in his ever-so-proper Edinburgh accent.

'*Mr Gillespie is consistently late for work on the early morning shifts and frequently argues with the local managers who point out his shortcomings in performance and attitude. He tends to be overfamiliar with distillery employees, which could seriously jeopardise the security of the Revenue and classified information. However, he is usually accurate in numerical work and writes clear reports.*'

Macalister paused and looked up at Tom. 'At least there is a bit of light amidst the dark,' he said.

He continued. '*However, his private life leaves much to be desired and is obviously affecting his official work. Gillespie is known to be a heavy drinker and takes little or no heed of the recently introduced regulations on drinking and driving. There are reports of him going through several sets of red lights in Aberdeen at around 4 a.m. in a black sports car accompanied by two passengers (female). Additionally, there are rumours that he crashed his car against a concrete lamp post. Surprisingly, there is no police report of this event nor of any injuries. This officer will have to mend his ways if he is to remain in the Service and prevent serious injury to himself and others.*

'It makes dismal reading,' said the controller as he closed the file. 'I have also heard informal but as yet unconfirmed reports of other incidents. Notably that you threatened to fight the chief inspector of lifeboats, of all people, in the Commercial Hotel at Buckie over some late-night argument on the respective merits of Speyside and Lowland whiskies. Also, that you were thrown out of your digs in Stonehaven after brawling with a group of Scottish Nationalists on the night that Celtic won the European Cup. Were these reports accurate?'

Tom knew that to deny them would be futile. It seemed as if Macalister's spies were everywhere. He chose to remain silent and gave a nervous cough.

'I thought so,' Macalister said with obvious annoyance. 'And now I have in front of me a request for permission to go on a holiday to the Soviet Union and visit other Communist countries en route. I am inclined to refuse your request. However, a month out of my hair is a pleasure I find impossible to resist. Perhaps in some mysterious way such an experience may help you to grow up and adopt a more responsible attitude to your behaviour.'

Tom inwardly breathed a sigh of relief. It looked as if the meticulous holiday plans they had made would not be in vain. But he knew the controller was not going soft. There was bound to be a catch, or stringent conditions.

Macalister cleared his throat and looked Tom straight in the eyes. His face was set like Aberdeen granite.

'You have no doubt read the instructions about travel to Communist countries?'

'Yes, sir,' Tom replied truthfully.

'You should also be aware from press reports that relations between East and West have not been good of late. Some Western businessmen and academics have been arrested by the Soviet authorities on trumped-up spying charges. They are then used as bargaining tools in negotiating the release of Soviet spies held in the West. You and your two friends could be at risk if you do not adhere strictly to the official guidelines.'

He then emphasised the main points again:

'No currency dealing.

'No fraternising with Soviet women.

'No departure from or argument with the visitors' conditions laid down by the Intourist Soviet Travel Agency.'

Then came the rapier thrust. 'I am also formally warning you now, Gillespie, that from today you will be on a disciplinary trial period for six months, which will include your holiday in the Soviet Union. Your recent poor work and behaviour have brought the Service into disrepute and need to be significantly improved. If I am not satisfied at the end of the period, you will be dismissed.' He paused, then said, 'That is all. You may go.'

Tom swallowed hard, grimaced and left the room.

Morag looked up from her desk as Tom came out and saw he wasn't smiling.

'Pretty rough, was it, Tom?' she whispered in a concerned voice.

'Yes. I'm for the chop in six months if I can't persuade the boss that I'm a reformed character.'

'Don't worry,' she said in a clucking tone. 'You will. I'll get you that cup of coffee now.'

Tom drank the hot, sweet coffee quickly, winked at Morag and left the building. He was glad to feel the warm July sunshine and the reassurance of the bustle and life of Union Street. He reflected briefly on the past hour in the cool humourless office in front of a dry, humourless man.

Boring old fart, he thought.

Tom was twenty-four years old, single, fit and healthy. The world was his oyster, and he was going to enjoy it.

4

Bernie

To say that Bernard Hugo Carleton was interested in cars would be as absurd as saying that Georgie Best was a reasonable footballer. Bernie, as he was universally known, was fanatical about cars. He ate, slept and drank cars. He drooled over them. He caressed and fondled their curves and shapes. He loved exploring their innermost regions, unlocking mysterious secrets, oiling strange parts, tweaking nipples. Pistons, pumps, big ends, little ends, gaskets, grommets and rpms were food and drink to him. These inanimate mechanical hard parts were to him the stuff of beauty and form. When the whole burst into life by the ignition magic of the internal combustion engine, it was like a scientific miracle.

He had learnt much from his dad, who used to tinker with the family car mainly to save on garage bills. But Bernie developed the lessons of necessity into the pleasures of virtue. On leaving school after A levels in Bristol, Bernie decided to study mechanical engineering at King's College, London, where he graduated with a first-class honours degree. However, during his student days, his fascination with the science of mechanics gradually gave way to model design, and in his final year he spent many a happy hour in the student union bar holding forth on the cars of the future.

Many of his contemporaries found his obsession profoundly boring and would far rather have argued the merits of Descartes and Kant, the musical differences of the Beatles and the Stones, or the effects of cannabis versus LSD than listen to what the next car was going to look like. Still, while ever Bernie was buying the drinks, he never lacked an audience. This relationship between free drink and captive audience should be cited as a general truism equal in status to the certainties of death and taxes.

Tom had met up with Bernie in London a year after Bernie had left King's in 1964. By chance they shared the same digs in Clapham and became firm friends. Such a friendship was unexpected. Bernie's passion for cars naturally fuelled an enthusiasm for motor sports, particularly rally driving. His crinkly black hair and tall, slim frame came with debonair good looks. Most women found him irresistible – which was a pity for them, since they invariably played second fiddle to Bernie's cars. But not always.

He had no interest in the popular more dominant sports of football, cricket and rugby – all of which Tom played and also followed from the terraces, the pub and the armchair. In politics they were at opposite ends of the spectrum. Genghis Khan was regarded by Bernie as a wimp, while Tom rejoiced in the vision of the new Labour Government. The prime minister's sound bite of the white heat of the technological revolution had defined the new politics.

The old order of Edwardian *noblesse oblige*, brilliantly exploited by Macmillan and, latterly, Sir Alec Douglas-Home, famous for his economic matchsticks, had disintegrated into sleaze, sexual scandal and incompetence. In the sixties a modern zeitgeist had arisen – times they were a-changing. But what the two friends had in common was travel and a sense of adventure that mirrored the spirit of the day. They had crossed the Alps together in 1965 driving an old banger on a journey to Rome and back. A trip to the Soviet Union a couple of years later seemed a natural choice.

Bernie knew time was passing quickly, and a meeting was needed to finalise the details of the journey.

Better phone up that waster in Aberdeen, he thought, and reached for his desk telephone. Ferrari (UK) Ltd would hardly call him to account for the occasional private phone call. He rang Tom's digs in Rosemount Terrace, Aberdeen, and spoke to Mrs McCrae.

'Is Tom there?' Bernie asked.

'No. He's been posted back to Huntly at short notice. I think he's in trouble at work. Mind you, I'm not surprised. He's out to all hours at night and looks dreadful in the mornings. Also, I'm sorry I don't know where he is staying in Huntly. Before he left, he muttered something about a new girlfriend. You know what he's like. Perhaps he'll be staying with her.'

'Thanks, Mrs McCrae,' said Bernie. 'I'll track him down.'

Perhaps Dunk knows where he is, he thought. *Now, what's that funny little town called where he's staying?* He flicked to the address pages at the back of his diary and read, *Duncan Matheson, c/o 21 Conval Street, Dufftown, Banffshire. Tel. Dufftown 684.*

He rang the number.

5

Dunk

Mrs George had just sat down for a quiet cup of tea to read the *Daily Record* in her front room when she heard the phone ring. She was a busy woman in her early fifties, of generous girth and cheerful disposition. The boarding house she ran in Dufftown was well known and very popular with the itinerant Excise officers who were constantly on the move around the Speyside distilleries. She and her husband, Harry, acted in a sort of unofficial way as *in loco parentis* to the young and mainly English officers who roamed about the Highlands. She had just the right blend of no-nonsense yet flexible discipline to keep an orderly house and control some of the wilder elements who passed through her doors.

'Och, I can see I'll nay gae much time tae maesel today,' she said, sighing as she heaved her not inconsiderable weight off the sofa and went to answer the phone in the hallway. 'Hello, this is Dufftown 684,' she said.

'Could I speak to Duncan Matheson, please?' asked Bernie in his slight Somerset drawl.

'I'll see if the loon's in,' said Mrs George, leaving Bernie to puzzle over the meaning of loon. No doubt it was a strange esoteric Scottishism used only by the local clan.

'It's another bloody foreign language,' he thought.

Mrs George went down the hallway to the back living room, where Duncan was sitting at the dining table reading *The Scotsman,* enjoying his elevenses with a couple of ginger biscuits and a mug of coffee.

'There's an English manny on the phone for ye, Dunk,' said Mrs George, who then went back to her tea and her paper.

Duncan Ian Matheson was of medium height, lean and very fit. After taking his MA in English at Aberdeen University he applied to Customs and Excise mainly as a stopgap so he could remain in the Highlands until he had decided exactly what he wanted to do. Contrary to his expectations, his first appointment had been to London Port. During his stay in various digs and flats in London, he had come to know Tom and Bernie. The three friends soon gained a widespread notoriety for giving wild all-night parties in their large flat just off Kilburn High Road and were regularly invited to other friends' parties. If the Triumvirate, as they became known, were there, people knew it would be a good night. However, the London scene came to an abrupt end for Dunk and Tom when they were posted to the East Scotland region in June 1966.

Dunk was a superb sportsman, who outshone his contemporaries in most games. His favourites were soccer, tennis and golf, but he was also a keen hill walker and fisherman. In fact, he was intending to try out his new salmon rod that evening on the River Fiddich. A recent spell of heavy rain had left the river in spate, enabling shoals of fighting salmon, which had been previously trapped in the pools near the estuary, to make their way up the river to their final spawning beds. He was optimistic of landing at least a good eight-pounder.

Another of Dunk's interests was shooting, both with rifle and handgun. He first became involved with this sport as a child when his parents took over the management of Altnacealgach, a Highland hotel in Sutherland, in the early 1950s. Along with his brother Ranald he would shoot rats, which were attempting to raid the hotel's hen coop, with a .22 rifle. He enjoyed the experience so much that as a teenager he joined a local gun club and became proficient enough to be able to enter shooting competitions.

He dunked another biscuit into his coffee and sucked on the sweet, spicy ginger biscuit, crunching into it as he went down the hallway to take the telephone call. It was hardly a mystery to work out the origins of his nickname. Duncan had been dunking his biscuits into hot drinks since the age of five. Twenty years later, the habit had become totally ingrained, as natural to him as breathing or blowing his nose.

'Dunk here,' he said in his quick Invernessian accent.

'Hello, Dunk,' said Bernie. 'How's things with you and Tom?'

'Great for me, but Tom's been in the proverbial again and has had a final bollocking from the boss. If he gets into any more trouble he's going to get the sack. He can be a right arse. It's as if he must have that element of risk in his life to give him a buzz.'

'Well, keep the bugger out of mischief at least until we set off to Russia. I tried to ring him at his Aberdeen address but was told that he had been sent to a place called Huntly. We need to have a final meeting to tie up the loose ends and to make sure we have all the necessary documents and route plans. I suggest York this Saturday.'

'Fine,' said Dunk. 'That's no problem for me. I'll go over and see Tom tonight and take him fishing. It's only about fifteen miles from here. I'll ring you back tomorrow, Bernie, and let you know about York.'

6

Who to Select?

The red telephone on the Foreign Secretary's desk broke the silence of the palatial office with its distinctive sharp ring. David Tompkins hesitated before he picked up the phone. He knew the call would be important. It would be either the prime minister himself or somebody with the express permission of the prime minister.

His appointment to the post at the last cabinet reshuffle seven months before had taken him by surprise. Although confident in his own abilities, he thought that his comparative youth, at the age of forty-one, would bar him for a few years from such a senior cabinet position. However, his success in his previous post as Secretary of State for the Environment, and before that as Minister of State for Europe, had not gone unnoticed.

Only once before had the red telephone rung – about four months ago, when the prime minister had asked for detailed, secret information on Franco–German policy before a cabinet meeting to consider an impending sterling crisis. The aftermath of that call, and subsequent meeting, were several all-night sittings in the House, two ministerial resignations and six weeks of strikes by public sector unions. Would this call mean that he would again have to bid farewell to his wife and young family for a few weeks and prop his eyes open with matchsticks? He picked up the phone.

'Hello, Foreign Secretary here,' he said.

'Could you please hold the line, Mr Tompkins? Sir Richard Temple will speak to you,' said the brisk but pleasant female voice of Jennifer Ashcroft.

'So it is national security,' he said to himself. Within seconds he was speaking to the head of the British security services.

'Good afternoon, Foreign Secretary,' said Sir Richard, who always observed the formalities of address when speaking by telephone to cabinet ministers, even if he knew them well.

'I met with the prime minister and the American ambassador this morning. We have a major problem with the Soviets and I need your help. As a result of George Blake's defection, all our agents in the Warsaw Pact countries have been exposed except one. I will be with you in about an hour to brief you, but in the meantime I would be obliged if you could recommend a suitable person in our Moscow, Budapest and Warsaw embassies who may be able to go undercover or else liaise with an inexperienced agent.

'Also, there is an Italian connection to this enterprise. I need a discreet contact in our embassy in Rome or within our Vatican Consulate. Finally, I need a list containing the personal details of all British nationals who have applied for a visa to visit the Soviet Union during the next two months.'

'Very good, Sir Richard. I look forward to seeing you soon and will have the information you require.'

David Tompkins put down the phone and looked out of

the large oblong window into the cloudless blue summer sky. Something very big and risky was afoot. He awaited Sir Richard's visit with eagerness but apprehension.

After making his call, the security chief considered his options as he chewed a ham sandwich at his desk. They were not good, and he needed time to think before making his way to Whitehall. He was in unchartered territory and was undecided about how much to tell Tompkins.

He arrived at the Foreign Office just as the chimes of Big Ben struck three and was immediately escorted to the Foreign Secretary's private office, where he was greeted personally by David Tompkins.

'Good afternoon, Sir Richard. Please come in. Would you like a cup of tea or coffee or perhaps something stronger?'

'Not yet, Foreign Secretary. Maybe later,' he said as he shook the outstretched hand and went to sit in the high-backed crimson-upholstered chair near to the ornate gold-framed portrait of Lord Halifax.

David Tompkins took his seat in the matching chair facing the spymaster with a beautifully crafted Queen Anne coffee table between them. He remained silent and waited for his guest to speak.

'You are aware that, six years ago, President Kennedy pledged that the USA would land a man on the Moon before the end of the decade?'

'Indeed,' replied Tompkins. 'After Kennedy's assassination, President Johnson pledged that NASA would have whatever funds were required to make this possible. As it happens, I was speaking to the US Secretary of State only two weeks ago at our embassy in Washington on this very subject. He was confident that the Moon mission was on target, with some scientists speculating that the event could take place in the autumn of 1968 – next year, although prudent estimates suggest the spring of the following year.'

'Well,' continued Sir Richard, 'the situation is now very different. Let me explain. The Soviets are determined to stop the US Moon landing or at least delay it until they have achieved it first. We know that their technology is at least five years behind that of the USA, but they could possibly land their man on the Moon by the early seventies. If this were to happen before the Americans, then Soviet international prestige would dominate the world overnight and provide enormous validation to the Soviet Communist system. Many of the newly emergent nations in Africa and Asia, as well as some of the more volatile South American countries, would look to Russia rather than the West for support and ideological leadership. We would face a political disaster if this were to happen.'

Sir Richard paused to see if the Foreign Secretary wished to comment. David Tompkins drew in his breath sharply, pursed his lips and fiddled nervously with his Rolex. He understood the scenario completely and said, 'Please continue.'

'After the last war, many of the best German rocket scientists were captured by Stalin's forces and were employed willingly or forcibly on the Soviet space programme. That is why they were the first to launch the Sputnik in 1957 and were able to beat the Americans with the first man in space, Yuri Gagarin, in 1961.

'Unfortunately for the West, the Russians still maintain booster rocket superiority. But, unfortunately for them, we have a reliable mole on their space development committee, who has been passing highly classified material on rocket science to us via our field agents. We have passed this over to the Americans, who have almost caught up with the Soviets in this particular area of space research.

'However, the loss of our agents through Blake's defection means that the remaining vital information that the Americans need in order to complete the rocket development for their Moon space mission is no longer available. Our only hope is to re-establish contact with our Russian mole who, we suspect, is under suspicion by the KGB, but who, so far, lack the evidence to arrest him.'

At this point Tompkins interrupted and said, 'I think it's time for that drink now – and I don't mean tea or coffee.'

Sir Richard gave a wry smile and nodded in agreement. 'Mine's a Scotch,' he said. 'A large one.'

7

A Surprise Candidate

The minister went over to the rosewood cabinet and took out two Caithness crystal glasses. He put them on the antique Georgian silver tray that occupied a nearby small table and reached inside the cabinet again for the matching decanter, which was two thirds-full of eighteen-year-old Glenlivet. He then went over to his desk, picked up the internal phone and said, 'Jonathan, please bring me a small jug of iced water.'

He took the tray over to the Queen Anne coffee table and, with a knowing smile at Sir Richard, poured out three fingers into both glasses, saying, with a knowing wink, 'I know you like your malt with a dash of water. Foreign Secretaries also have their spies.'

Sir Richard raised his glass and smiled approval and acknowledgement. He took a sip of the mellow amber liquid while waiting for the water. It was David Tompkins who returned to their discussions.

'I entirely agree with the political consequences of your analysis. I could go further and explain the likely effects with our allies in Europe – but that's another discussion. You presumably have some plan to re-establish contact with the Russian mole?'

There was a knock on the door. Tompkins stood up

and walked across the Afghan carpet, which had been a personal gift from the Emperor Haile Selassie to Ernest Bevin, and took the jug of water from his private secretary.

'Thank you, Jonathan. Could you also bring me the files I asked for earlier?'

'I have them in my office ready for you, Minister, with recommendations. Shall I put them on your desk?'

'Please,' said Tompkins, and returned to his seat with the water. How pleasant were the perks and privileges of power – particularly efficient, obedient and very civil servants.

Sir Richard poured a dash of water into his glass, took a sip, added a mere sensation more, sipped again and said, 'Perfect,' then continued.

'We now have no trained agents working inside the Soviet Union, except one. We also suspect that Blake is not the last of the Cambridge traitor network recruited by Burgess and Maclean, and that there is at least one other highly placed agent within our own British establishment. The information in your files should provide details on diplomatic staff in certain Communist countries who may be suitable to assist an agent. However, their personal details of accreditation will be known to the other side and would thus debar them from active work as an undercover agent. The initiative at the moment is with the Soviets, and all our embassy staff will be watched like hawks.'

He paused for a long drink of his malt, as if he needed to flush the audacity of his decision out of his brain. Tompkins said nothing but awaited expectantly, knowing the chief had come to the heart of the matter.

'I intend to select a complete unknown for this job. The person will be briefed and trained within the next two months. We do not have the luxury of time. But at least the Soviets do not know who the person is. Nor does anybody else, for that matter.

'Indeed, neither do I, for no selection has yet been made. That is why I need to know who has been granted visas to travel to Russia within the next three months. Existing applications would have been granted before the Blake revelations and would not attract suspicion, as any new ones would.'

The minister read the summary paper, stroked his top lip with his thumb and forefinger and grimaced.

'It's a risky business. There are only fifty-two people on this visa list. Forty-three of them are MPs, embassy visitors, academics and British Communist Party members, who are all well known to the Soviets. The remaining nine are holidaymakers. You will therefore have a very limited base to make your choice from. Have you not considered someone from MI6 or Special Branch? They would be fully trained in all the skills required by your own agents, positively vetted and physically very fit.'

'Yes, I have considered that option, but dismissed it. All such officers are known to Home Office and Foreign Office ministers and their permanent secretaries. We cannot be sure that Blake or the suspected British mole has not passed this information to the Russians. A complete unknown is the only way.'

'I understand,' said Tompkins. 'Here are the files you wanted on the embassies and visa applications. I would be grateful if you would let me know who you select.'

Sir Richard drained his glass, savouring the last drops of this excellent Scotch. He stood up and put the files into his briefcase.

'Thank you, Foreign Secretary, for your time and information – and especially the drink. I shall return these files as soon as I have finished with them. On Saturday I am due to see the prime minister to give him details of my plan and selections. It will be his decision about who else should be told.'

The significance of this latter remark was not lost on David Tompkins. He nodded and walked over to open his office door. He shook his visitor warmly by the hand and said, 'Good luck. You certainly will need it.'

8

An Old Flame

Within fifteen minutes the security chief was back at his desk. He took out the files from his briefcase and carefully examined them. The forty-three official visitors were examined first to see if any would be suitable for the mission. However, their public identities ruled them out. The remaining nine holidaymakers were his last chance. Two were a newly married couple, obviously looking for a memorable honeymoon in what they thought would be an exotic country. They would obviously have more pressing matters to think about without the distractions of a highly dangerous and secret operation. Three others were all single young men heading for Yalta on the Black Sea in an old Ford convertible.

Bloody daft, he thought. Such a distance was bound to wreck the car, if Russian petrol didn't do so first. The remaining four were a family of a mother, a father and two teenage girls of Jewish–Russian descent visiting relatives for the first time in Smolensk. The father's father had been deported by Stalin in the pogroms of the 1930s and murdered at some remote labour camp, but other family members had managed to escape to a nearby forest and survived. Even if the father was willing to do the job, his background would ensure that the Soviet authorities kept him under surveillance while visiting his Russian family.

What a bloody useless bunch, he thought, and stared blankly at the papers before him sensing that depressing feeling of failure. Then there was a tap on his door.

'Come in,' Sir Richard said wearily. Jennifer Ashcroft entered, looking stunning in a pale blue miniskirt and cream chiffon blouse. Her auburn hair fell in ringlets onto her shoulders. The light and sweet allure of Chanel No. 5 was her perfect choice of perfume. She looked cool and in command, but sensuous.

He brightened up immediately and mentally regretted his recent neglect of his dedicated assistant.

'I thought you might like a coffee,' she said, and smiled at him.

'Fine. You must have read my thoughts, Jennifer,' he replied. The stimulation of the Glenlivet had now worn off and had made him thirsty. He would certainly welcome a dose of caffeine.

Jennifer returned carrying a tray with a jug of piping hot Columbian coffee, a plain white china bowl of demerara sugar and Sir Richard's favourite coffee mug, showing a salmon leaping up a highland waterfall. On the tray was also a small white plate etched with a tartan pattern round the edge, on which were placed two Dean's shortbread biscuits. She placed the tray on the right-hand side of his desk, poured out the coffee, put in two spoonfuls of the brown sugar, stirred it and placed the mug on the ornamental circular place mat made of jade just below the desk telephone. She looked at Sir Richard, smiled again and said, 'Will there be anything else, sir?'

'Not at the moment,' he said, but allowed himself a

fleeting image of a later, less formal meeting.

He took a long drink of the coffee and then looked anew at the papers before him. Suddenly, something caught his eye: *He has served for the past four years in various parts of the UK with HM Customs and Excise.* This was in the papers, and it described the three young male holidaymakers.

He reread the file again and his interest was aroused. There was the hint of a possibility. He read an insert from the Customs Personnel Directorate.

Gillespie travelled extensively in Europe after leaving university, where he graduated with a 2:1 in modern languages. He spent a year at the University of Rome. He speaks fluent Italian and has a very good grasp of French and German. He has been recommended for a post in our European Tariff Section but opted for a two-year stint in Aberdeen Collection. His disciplinary record is poor, yet he is intelligent and resourceful. He is due for a career and posting appraisal in six months.

'This Gillespie seems to be an undisciplined maverick, a risk-taker who also speaks Italian, as does Dante. I think I'll have a chat with him, face to face.'

Sir Richard picked up his desk phone. 'Jennifer, get me the chairwoman of Customs and Excise, Veronica Johnson.'

He knew Veronica from their early days together at the Board of Trade. They had both been junior civil servants in their early twenties and had been recognised as high-fliers within the class-ridden structures of Whitehall preferment. They were moved around different departments, along with other hopefuls, to give them a broad experience of the machinery of government, as it was grandly termed.

Veronica had done very well, rising through the ranks at

the Board of Trade with two successful stints in the Home Office and the Inland Revenue before her appointment as chairwoman of Customs and Excise at the comparatively early age of forty-three. In fact, their relationship was more than a good friendship. They had had a brief affair about ten years ago, but Veronica had reluctantly ended it when her father accidentally found out and threatened to tell her husband if she did not stop. The collapse of her marriage and the loss of custody of her two children was a risk she was not prepared to take.

The phone rang, and Richard Temple heard Veronica's voice for the first time in several years.

'Richard, how lovely to hear from you. How are you?' she said in her soft-spoken voice.

Sir Richard's pulse quickened as he exchanged pleasantries with his ex-lover. She could still get under his skin, but he liked it. After a few minutes of catching up on personal news, she said archly, 'I'm sure that after such a long time this is not entirely a social call from the head of our security services on a protected outside line, is it?'

'You are quite right, Veronica,' he said. 'You have an officer called Gillespie currently serving in your Highland region. He is going to the Soviet Union next month with two other friends – one of whom also works for you up there. Matheson is his name.

'I need to speak to Gillespie as soon as possible. From his personnel records he is due a career interview in six months' time. I want you to bring that forward for this Friday, the day after tomorrow, but say nothing about my involvement. You can make up some realistic excuse about a new project in European tax harmonisation or a disciplinary hearing. Say anything you like, but get him to King's Beam House by 11 a.m. on Friday morning. I will see him there in your office. Also, I want to examine both his and Matheson's detailed personnel files. For the record, this matter is specifically authorised by the prime minister.'

Like all permanent secretaries, Veronica Johnson would have been positively vetted and knew that whatever the security services needed you gave them. And you never asked questions. You did as you were told.

'Very well, Richard. The files will be delivered to you by courier within the hour, and rest assured that Gillespie will be here on Friday.' She paused and then continued in a lighter tone. 'Perhaps we may manage lunch together?'

'Perhaps,' he said. He thanked her for her cooperation, although she had no choice, and put the phone down.

It was now late. It had been a long day and he was tired. Once the files arrived there would be nothing else he could usefully do. He would call it a day.

9

A Trip to London

At 9.15 a.m. prompt, Miss Teesdale brought in the controller's coffee along with the *Aberdeen Press and Journal,* or, to give it its colloquial title, the *Depress and Jumpnow,* due to its relentless reportage of deaths, crime and the sordid, unseemly side of human nature.

Robert Macalister was in a good mood. It had been a fine, sunny weekend and he had won the golf championship at his local club. Also, the latest statistics for his region were impressive, so perhaps he would be considered for a further promotion – the post of UK Director Outfield was soon to become vacant.

He opened the paper and began to scan the front page. An item just below the main headline of a multiple car crash between Stonehaven and Laurencekirk caught his eye. *Is the De'il awa' wi' the exciseman?*

He read, *Yesterday, Huntly police arrested exciseman Mr T. Gillespie, who allegedly was caught red-handed by Baillie Malcolm McBain fishing the private waters of the Castle Hotel on the River Deveron. Gillespie's accomplice got away, but police are continuing their enquiries. A ten-pound salmon, two sea trout, two fishing rods and a bag of tackle were all confiscated. Gillespie, a temporary resident of Greenmount, Gordon Street, will appear before the Sheriff in Elgin on Wednesday.*

The shout of anger from Macalister startled Miss Tees. She had never seen her boss so irate. 'What's the matter?' she said, with growing concern.

'That bloody fool Gillespie has landed himself in court for poaching on the Deveron. Look – it's front-page news in the *P & J*.'

By now, Macalister's mood had completely changed. He knew exactly what he was going to do. Only a few weeks ago he had warned Gillespie about his behaviour. This was the last straw. He had to go. He picked up his phone and rang Jim Morton, his staff appointments officer. 'Where's Gillespie?' he barked.

'Kennethmont, sir,' said Morton.

'Replace him immediately and get him back here. I want to see him by eleven o'clock in my office.'

'Very good, sir,' replied Morton. He also had read the *P &J* and guessed what was coming.

The call to the distillery was answered by Ewan, the brewer. 'Can you get Tom Gillespie to the phone?' said Jim Morton. 'It's the collector's office here.'

'Hello, Jim. Tom's in the filling store, so I'll transfer your call there. We've all been pulling his plonker over his salmon poaching. I presume you know it's all over the *P & J*. Don't expect your boss is very happy.'

'Too damn right, Ewan,' said Jim, and waited for the call to be transferred.

Tom answered the phone. 'Macalister wants you in his office by eleven this morning. Sandy MacAfee will be arriving shortly to take over. I expect you can guess what it's about.'

There was a short pause at the other end of the line. 'Yes,' said Tom. 'He's going to promote me.'

'You've got it in one,' said Jim continuing the grim humour. 'Promotion to the unemployment benefit office.'

Robert Macalister had just completed dictating the dismissal letter when his direct line phone rang. It was Veronica Johnson.

'Good morning, Robert, and how are things with you?' After the usual pleasantries typical between subordinates and superiors, the chairwoman came to the point of the call. 'I understand you have an officer in your region called Gillespie.'

Macalister could hardly believe his ears. Surely London hadn't heard of Gillespie's antics. After all, this was a local matter. The chairwoman would have bigger fish to fry.

'Yes, ma'am,' answered Macalister, intrigued as to what was likely to come next, and why such high-profile interest.

'Well, I need him here in London by tomorrow morning for a special briefing. There is a particular job required in negotiations with the European Community. Gillespie's background and qualifications make him the ideal candidate to assist our tax harmonisation team.'

'There could be a problem with releasing him in such a short time. And also his suitability for such a responsible job is very doubtful,' said Macalister. He then proceeded to outline Gillespie's poor performance, behaviour and imminent court appearance.

But Veronica Johnson was adamant. 'I don't care what sort of trouble he is in. Get an adjournment of his court case, pay his bail and make sure he is in London by 11 a.m. tomorrow.'

Macalister was dumbfounded. However, he knew better than to argue with his boss. After all, she had the power to make or break him, and he was desperate for a further promotion. 'Very good, ma'am. I'll ensure that he catches the London sleeper tonight.'

The controller then grimaced, whistling through his teeth, and called his secretary. 'Cancel that dismissal notice on Gillespie, Morag. It would seem that our poacher has a powerful protector and some European friends, as well as the luck of the Devil.'

At 11 a.m. Tom arrived at the controller's office, fearing the worst. He had taken the precaution of collecting all his belongings from his digs in Huntly in anticipation of receiving his P45. He smiled wanly at Morag before going in to see Macalister. 'Well, darling, it looks as if we will have to put our night of passion on hold for a bit longer,' he said.

Morag smiled sweetly and seductively. 'I don't know about that,' she said. 'I think you're in for quite a surprise.'

Tom went in to see a stony-faced Macalister, who was sitting with his hands crossed over a neatly arranged desk. He prepared himself for the worst. 'You are one of the worst officers under my command, and if it were up to me you would be instantly dismissed. However, you are to report to the chairwoman of the board personally at 11 a.m. tomorrow. Something to do with a job in Europe.

'Make sure you are on the overnight train, arrive there sober and … good riddance.'

10

Bogdan Demiuk

Bogdan Demiuk had returned to his native Ukraine in 1965 after several years in both the UK and Italy. He had taken a master's degree in aviation studies at Cambridge University and had gained practical experience at BAE Systems in Bristol. His time in Italy had been mainly a personal indulgence, since he was very interested in Italian literature, especially Dante. However, it also had given him the opportunity to meet up with his brother, who at that time was studying to be a priest at the National Ukrainian College in Rome.

While at Cambridge, he had been approached by MI6 to work as a British agent when he returned to the Soviet Union. At first Bogdan was not interested, since he had little time for politics and had devoted his career to aviation. Gradually, however, he became intellectually convinced that the Soviet system was totally corrupt and the Communist economic system unworkable. The crimes perpetrated by Stalin in the years of terror during the 1930s, 1940s and 1950s had recently been made public by the General Secretary, Nikita Khrushchev. Bogdan, along with millions of other Soviet citizens, was appalled. He realised that Western democracies, though not perfect, were more economically successful and open, and were better guarantors of people's freedom.

He decided to contact MI6 to explain his change of mind, but was surprised by what the then chief, Sir Richard Temple, proposed. On his return home, Sir Richard said, he wanted him to get a post in the Soviet Space Agency. Bogdan's background at Cambridge and Bristol, together with his knowledge of British aviation, would be of great advantage to the Soviets. He was instructed to do nothing other than obtain as much information as he could about Soviet space intentions, and particularly rocket technology.

A secret bank account was arranged, and he was to lie dormant until contacted. His contact name would be Dante, one Bogdan had chosen himself, and would only be known to the chief himself.

As expected, Demiuk was welcomed by the Soviet Space Agency, and was soon able to secure a transfer to specialise in rocket development. Within two years he had established himself as a respected authority within that specialism. He had never once been contacted by Sir Richard, and he continued to enjoy the funds from the private bank account. These funds were periodically topped up from an address in Rome, where he was able to access the account when visiting his brother.

He was aware that George Blake had escaped from Wormwood Scrubs prison the year before and had finally arrived in Moscow. Nevertheless, he was confident that his identity had not been compromised since no one knew who he was, except the chief himself.

Then, at the beginning of August 1967, Demiuk received his first coded message via his bank account. It said that at some time within the next two weeks he would meet a young Englishman named Tom on the beach in Yalta. It also said that Tom spoke fluent Italian and would be with two friends.

Demiuk would be asked to provide highly classified information about the Soyuz rocket programme. The first item of this code would be a book title and the second would be information in letters and numbers relating to the book, for deciphering the contents of the code. This document was to be given to his brother, Joseph, who was to personally hand it to the rector of the English College in Rome. Demiuk was to await his instructions and be fully aware that the situation was dangerous but necessary.

Bogdan Demiuk let out a long low whistle. 'So the die is cast,' he said to himself. 'I wonder what plans London is pursuing?'

He felt a single trickle of sweat roll down his neck, but gave a shrug and returned to his office.

11

Meeting With the Chairwoman

As instructed, Tom presented himself at 10.45 a.m. on the dot at King's Beam House, the head office of HM Customs and Excise. It was a purpose-built office block, not much different from hundreds of similar buildings in London.

He introduced himself to the doorkeeper, who consulted his list of appointments. His eyebrows raised when he saw that Tom had an appointment with Veronica Johnson herself.

'You are expected, sir,' the doorkeeper said, 'and I am to escort you personally to her office.'

They took the lift to the fourth floor and approached a solid oak door with a simple plaque on the front that read: *Veronica Johnson, Chairwoman of HM Customs and Excise,* with the crest of the department just below her name and title. The doorkeeper knocked on the door.

'Come in,' said a clear female voice.

The doorkeeper entered, with Tom a step behind.

'This is Mr Thomas Gillespie, here for the meeting with you at 11 a.m., ma'am.'

'Thank you, Bill,' she said, 'and welcome to you, Mr Gillespie.' She extended her hand, which Tom shook firmly.

'Please come in. There is someone else here who I wish you to meet,' she said.

Tom could see a tall, slim man in a pinstriped suit who was gazing out of the window at the ebb and flow of traffic and people below. The chairwoman said, 'Mr Gillespie, let me introduce you to Sir Richard Temple, the head of MI6.'

Tom had no idea why he had been called to London. He had assumed that his fluency in Italian and good knowledge of French may have had something to do with a liaison post dealing with the European Economic Community, or perhaps an embassy appointment. But this was not at all what he was expecting: a top-level meeting with the head of Customs and Excise and the head of MI6.

Bloody hell, he thought. *What's all this about?*

'Tom,' Veronica began, then paused and said, 'I hope you don't mind me calling you Tom.'

'Not at all, ma'am,' said Tom.

'Good. I presume you are wondering why you have come to London for this meeting.'

Too right, thought Tom, but simply answered, 'Yes, ma'am.'

'I will let Sir Richard put you in the picture. However, before we commence, I must warn you that nothing about this meeting is to go beyond these four walls. You are still bound by the Official Secrets Act, which you signed on joining the department. You understand me, Tom?'

'Of course,' said Tom, and turned to face Sir Richard, who motioned him to sit down in one of the chairwoman's comfortable chairs.

Veronica Johnson sat down and gave Tom a reassuring smile. The MI6 boss remained standing and began to pace slowly around the room.

Sir Richard began. 'I understand that you and two

friends are going to the Soviet Union for a holiday. I commend your sense of adventure. It beats camping in the Lake District any day.'

Tom said nothing, but nodded agreement and waited for the spymaster to continue. Sir Richard stopped pacing the room and directly faced Tom.

'You may have heard that last year a Soviet spy called George Blake escaped from Wormwood Scrubs and has successfully reached Moscow, helped by associates here. Also, a few years ago, another British traitor, Kim Philby, the former head of UK relations with the American CIA, defected to the Soviets. These defections have cost the West dear, so much so that there are no longer any British nor US operatives within the Warsaw Pact. They have all been captured and executed except one, who is only known personally to me.

'This agent is a top scientist in the Soviet Space Agency. He goes under the code name of Dante. He speaks excellent English and good Italian. He has a brother living in Rome and a passion for Italian literature, hence his code name. I need to get an urgent message from him. This is where you and your friends are to be involved. As young, innocent tourists you have the perfect cover to successfully carry out a simple plan.' Sir Richard paused to let what he had said sink in.

Tom looked at the chairwoman, who inclined her head, then at Sir Richard.

'It's a big ask,' Tom said. 'Neither I nor my friends have any espionage experience. And there is no time for any training, since we go in six weeks.'

'That is precisely why you are perfect for the job,'

answered Sir Richard. 'All you need to do is obtain a message and collect an envelope. Nothing could be simpler. The only caveat is that you cooperate fully with the Soviet tourist agency, Intourist. All foreigners are monitored by the Soviet secret services, so any deviation from your approved route would cause suspicion and initiate surveillance.

'Dante will tell you the name of a book that is essential in deciphering his code. Even I do not know the name of this book. You are to remember it and not write it down. The code will have been given to his brother, Joseph, who is studying to be a priest in Rome. Dante goes to see his brother occasionally. The Soviet authorities are aware of this and, so far, have raised no objection.'

'If this code is with his brother in Rome, how will you get hold of it?' interjected Tom.

'Ah,' said Sir Richard. 'This is the second part of the operation, which I want you and your friends to help with. When you arrive in Vienna on your return journey I want you to go south to Rome, instead of making your way back to Calais. Dante's letter will be held by the rector of the English College, Monsignor James Burke. From your personnel file, I know that you spent time as a student there in the early sixties. Also, that you drove to Rome and back two years ago with your friend, Bernie. The Vatican and the English Church authorities have agreed to this arrangement. Neither have a clue what the letter contains, only that it is of major importance to the British government.'

Tom frowned, pursed his lips and said, 'You realise that this will mean a significant departure from our original plan. Presumably extra money and annual leave will be forthcoming to successfully accomplish this.'

'That will not be a problem,' replied Sir Richard. 'You will be allowed a grant of £500 to cover expenses, and a further month of annual leave to drive to Rome and return here. Part of that extra leave will be needed for a full debriefing.'

Veronica Johnson nodded in agreement. 'I will inform Mr Macalister that you and your friend, Mr Matheson, are to spend more time here in London later this month. I will also contact Mr Peterson, who is the head of office for your other friend, Mr Carleton, with the same information.'

I bet Macalister will be pleased, thought Tom. *I'm not exactly his shot of whisky at present.*

'Now,' said Sir Richard, 'I need your full consent to this operation. Do I have it?'

'Yes. I assume my two friends would also agree, but no doubt you will be seeing them,' said Tom.

'Of course. Within the next few days. But I want you to be the principal contact. Your plans may have to be changed quickly due to circumstances. You will have the final say.'

'Fine,' said Tom.

'One more point before we finish. You will certainly attract the attention of the KGB just because you are foreign and travelling widely in the USSR. As young men you will very likely be targeted by an attractive young woman or women. She will ask questions and will want to know about your trip. So, be careful what you say and do. Be friendly, yes. But intimate, no. Consensual sex can easily be interpreted as rape, and blackmail can be used with devastating effect.'

Tom raised his eyebrows and nodded. 'A honeytrap.

Point taken.'

'That is all for the time being,' said the spymaster. 'When I have spoken to your two friends a final meeting will take place here. You are to return on tonight's sleeper to Aberdeen and resume your Excise duties at Kennethmont, Ardmore Distillery for the next two weeks. If asked about your time here, you are to say that it concerns a posting to the European Economic Community, and you will be going to Brussels in three weeks' time for a trial period. There are times in this business when we have to be economical with the truth. I will see you in three weeks. Goodbye and thank you.'

Sir Richard held out his hand, which Tom warmly shook. Veronica Johnson did the same and squeezed Tom's hand as he was leaving. 'We have every confidence in you,' she said.

Tom took the Tube to King's Cross, booked his ticket and then went for a meal and a pint. He had a lot to think about.

12

The Journey Begins

The friends left Tom's house in Chesterfield at 4 a.m. and took the M1 to London. It was a clear night and the Ford convertible, which was nicknamed Lara, after the heroine in *Doctor Zhivago*, was running well. First, they had to visit the Polish and Soviet embassies to collect visas. Then, they headed south-east from the capital to meet the M2 for Dover and the ferry for Ostend.

After an uneventful crossing, which they spent relaxing pleasantly over a few beers, they reached their first campsite. This was situated about ten miles from Bruges, next to an attractive lake. They arrived at midnight, exhausted, erected the tent as quickly as possible and were soon fast asleep in their sleeping bags.

The next day was 1 August, Dunk's birthday, so they celebrated by opening a tin of grapefruit. The friends knew how to party. At around 4 p.m. they arrived at the West German border after an uneventful drive through Belgium. It was only a week since the meeting with the head of MI6, but they had not spoken much about it. They had been preoccupied with the details of their journey.

Now that they were en route, it was to dominate their conversation for the next few days. What were the dangers? Could this remaining contact, code-named Dante, be trusted? And why was the meeting to be in Yalta and not Moscow or some other Russian city? Why was the second part of the information to come via Rome? That was a considerable extra journey, which they had not expected nor planned.

So what was the deal, the reward? Promotion? A big fat cheque? Or many years in a Soviet gulag, if caught? Or a bullet in the back of the head?

They mulled over these questions for hours but decided there was no point in scaring themselves witless by concentrating on what might go wrong. In one sense it was an honour to have been chosen for this operation. Despite their youth, their superiors must have concluded that they had the intelligence and resilience to complete this mission successfully.

Being in Yalta would make matters a lot clearer. The contact would make himself known by using the word Dante in his conversation. He would suggest a book to be used in conjunction with a code. This code would be obtained at the English College in Rome.

'Bloody hell,' said Tom. 'It sounds like a James Bond plot.' The comparison was not so ridiculous.

They continued the journey driving through the night and arrived at Marienbad on the East German border. The entry formalities were completed without a problem. They were then able to drive along another of Hitler's autobahns to West Berlin. It was not difficult to see why many Germans idolised the Führer during the 1930s. He gave them work, stabilised the currency, and restored self-respect after the humiliation of the Treaty of Versailles. His darker, destructive side was then little known.

The city was very impressive. Indeed, it was beautiful. Bernie was shattered after his long drive, so Dunk and Tom went to a local flower market to exchange money and to check the route to Checkpoint Charlie, the border post from West Berlin to East Germany.

No problems were encountered on arrival at the Western checkpoint. However, after crossing no man's land to the East German side, the bureaucratic Iron Curtain came down with a clang. Since their visas said a different exit route, they had to go there, where everything was meticulously checked: passport, visas, driving licences and the contents of the car. Time was not a problem for the uniformed guard who was conducting the examination. It was as if he suspected the three of them were spies or at least mischief-makers. After what seemed like an age, the car and the papers were returned, and they set off for the Polish border.

Sterling needed to be exchanged at the border office in Poland for zlotys, at a ridiculously low exchange rate. This was proved not long after leaving the border, when a man emerged from some nearby bushes and stood directly on the road in front of the car. Fortunately for him, the car was being driven very slowly by Dunk, who was able to make an emergency stop.

'You stupid sod,' he shouted. 'You could have got yourself killed.'

This outburst of English made no impression on the man. He had a wad of zlotys in his hands and shouted, 'Sterling, sterling.' He offered five times the rate of exchange that they had got at the border post. Naturally a deal was done, despite the prohibitions of their superiors in London.

That night they camped in Poznań and slept for about eleven hours. On the next day the drive to Warsaw was without incident, but the sun was burning hot – weather they were having to get used to.

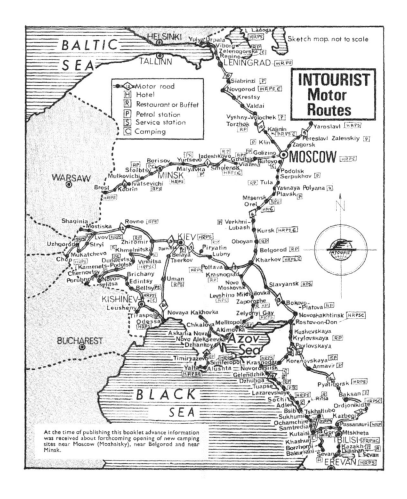

INTOURIST Motor Routes

Sketch map, not to scale

Motor road
H Hotel
R Restaurant or Buffet
P Petrol station
S Service station
C Camping

At the time of publishing this booklet advance information was received about forthcoming opening of new camping sites near Moscow (Mozhaisky), near Belgorod and near Minsk.

13

From Warsaw to Minsk and Moscow

They left Warsaw around noon, having used up all their zlotys on beer and goulash, and crossed the border into the USSR at 5.30 p.m. Here a smartly dressed Intourist guide checked them in. The Russian customs officers were very friendly and helpful when they learnt of their occupations. However, they were told that there was no camping site in Brest, which meant an exceptionally long drive of 250 kilometres through the night to Minsk. To add to their difficulties, they overshot the camping site and had to ask for directions at a hotel in the town centre at 2.30 in the morning.

As they drove towards the Minsk camping site they were pulled in by the police and all their equipment and documents were thoroughly checked. This was something they had to get used to while in the USSR.

They arrived at the site at 4.30 a.m. and had a mug of soup each before collapsing into their sleeping bags. They were up again at the crack of noon, with Tom and Bernie feeling rough, but the irrepressible Dunk playing a game of football with some Russian lads. The weather was extremely hot and humid.

'How does he do it?' asked Bernie as he crunched an apple, looking at Dunk through bleary eyes.

'Fuck knows,' said Tom. 'Must be in his Highland blood.'

The campsite had excellent facilities, particularly for washing and cooking. After lazing around for most of the day, they decided to get some vigorous exercise by playing a game of volleyball with some French lads. In the evening, they went to check out a local motel. Bernie decided to borrow Dunk's Matheson kilt, which caused a sensation as he approached the bar.

The motel was hosting an event for students who were obviously learning English. The friends were surrounded and questioned continuously about life back in the UK. The kilted Bernie, however, was monopolised by a beautiful young woman who said she was a chemistry professor at the Minsk Institute. Dunk was a little peeved, for while he and Tom were besieged by a multitude of questions from eager students, Bernie was, in Dunk's words, being made love to by this sexually incandescent Russian lass. He was obviously regretting not wearing his kilt and exploiting its riveting appeal to the opposite sex.

The following day they left Minsk with some reluctance and drove to Smolensk. Here the campsite was much inferior to the one at Minsk, with fewer facilities and a malodourous whiff of something very unpleasant. Still, it was sufficient for their needs. By the next day they should be in Moscow and hopefully enjoy a much better campsite.

14

Moscow

They arrived in Moscow in the late afternoon and found the Majestic camping site without difficulty. It overlooked the city's suburbs, which contained large soulless apartment blocks. It was the best site so far – clean, spacious with plenty of facilities. The car needed urgent repair due to a leaking oil pump. Bernie, ably assisted by Dunk, applied his prodigious mechanical knowledge and fixed it. After a meticulous service of its essential parts, the car was pronounced A1 by a triumphant Bernie. So they were able to explore the Russian capital.

At first, they strolled around the Kremlin wall eating the superb local ice cream that they bought from a picturesque kiosk, which provided several different flavours. Then to Red Square and finally to GUM. This was a three-storied domed department store. They spent about an hour there, and Dunk and Tom bought Cossack fur hats. People were generally very friendly, and they laughed and pointed at the fur hats. There was the occasional English speaker who wanted to know where they came from and whether they were enjoying Moscow. A resounding 'Yes,' with a thumbs up was the answer.

On returning to the campsite, they decided to enjoy a feast of cod roe, steak and champagne, which they had purchased en route before entering Russia. This did not seem to go down too well with some of the other visitors – especially a group of bearded English 'Ban the Bomb' supporters. Presumably, they were just jealous at seeing their fellow countrymen tuck into a gourmet meal while they chewed on fatty Russian sausages and stale bread.

The next day the friends were accompanied by Helena, an Intourist guide. She was of ample size but had a mournful face. Despite cracking jokes for her benefit, she remained impassive. Still, she spoke good English, which was all that mattered. She took them to see the New Virgin Nunnery, with its adjacent church and cemetery. Here lay the mortal remains of Stalin, his wife and the famous Russian playwright, Chekhov. For lunch they decided to push the boat out and visit the National Hotel, which was situated near the centre of the city. Here, a feast of caviar, Moscow soup (borsch), chicken steaks à la Kiev, ice cream and fruit, wine, cognac and coffee was thoroughly enjoyed and appreciated. Another surprise came when the bill arrived: everything for the princely sum of two pounds and ten shillings (£2.50 in decimal currency).

They then decided to go to a nearby Metro station, which was impressive in its spaciousness and marble walls, and to visit GUM again. Here, Bernie, not wishing to be outdone, bought a Cossack hat. There was a superb selection of postage stamps and postcards so, mindful of their families and friends back home, the friends bought plenty of each. Back at the site, the From Russia with Love greetings were sent to their sceptical contacts. Many of them had said that it would be a miracle if they got to Moscow, let alone return safely to the UK.

On the last day in Moscow, they went to the Kremlin Armoury and Museum. These housed the treasures of the former tsars and were mind-boggling in their opulence.

The Coronation Throne was encrusted with 870 diamonds and the Crown with 2,000. There were also many other exquisite artefacts, including a clock by Maddocks of England. They said to each other that it was not surprising that a revolution had taken place fifty years ago. Such a chasm of wealth between the monarch, the aristocracy and the comfortable middle class compared with the Russian working class and the serfs had made change – sadly, violent change – inevitable.

After saying goodbye to Helena, who had chaperoned them well around the major sites of Moscow, they returned to camp.

They decided to have an early dinner and to drive back into the city to take in the sites of Moscow at night. The car was parked near Gorky Street, which seemed to be a popular place for prostitutes. Here, the friends were approached by two prostitutes offering very reasonable rates for their services. However, not knowing their history, nor anything about these ladies of the night, their offers were politely refused.

Instead, they made for the ring road and arrived at the Exhibition of Economic Achievement – a sobering experience after the encounter with the ladies of pleasure. Then a motoring problem curtailed any further exploration of Moscow's night life. One of the car's tyres was flat, so they had to limp back to the campsite at a snail's pace in order not to damage the wheel any further. Since they were due to leave Moscow the next day, and anticipated a 5 a.m.

start, they agreed to have an early night.

It would not be long now before they arrived in Yalta. They hoped nothing had happened to Dante to jeopardise their mission and endanger their own lives. Had he been arrested by the KGB? But such negative thinking was not helpful. It would only increase their anxiety.

They dismissed these fears and settled down for the night. Yalta would reveal the outcome either way.

15

Gudenov, Head of the Russian KGB

It had been unfortunate for Roger Fanshaw to be on George Blake's list when the latter had successfully arrived in Russia after his escape from England in 1966. Fanshaw, with the help of British intelligence, had been appointed as a visiting lecturer in biochemistry at Moscow University. He was also an accomplished field agent for MI6, but Blake's revelations put an end to that. He was captured within hours of his disclosure by the brutal agents of Gudenov, the director of the Russian KGB.

His face was now unrecognisable, but the interrogators knew how to extract the maximum amount of pain without causing loss of consciousness or death, although sometimes this could not be guaranteed. Blood trickled down in a red, sticky stream from his eyes and nose into his mouth.

'The name, Comrade, the name,' demanded Godunov, 'and you will feel no more pain.'

'I don't know,' slurred Fanshaw in a hoarse, croaky voice.

'Then we shall have to jog your memory once more,' said Godunov, and nodded to his assistant, Rostov, to administer the electric shock treatment. He never got his hands dirty himself – just gave the orders to subordinates. But Rostov was different. He enjoyed the hands-on part of his job. He was a sadist.

The electric treatment applied to his testicles was excruciatingly painful. Fanshaw screamed out in agony and promptly vomited. He did not know the identity of his contact, only the female voice and the meeting place. But to end the pain he had to give them a name. Any name would have to do.

'Natasha Voranski,' he croaked.

'The deputy director of European operations in the KGB?' said Gudenov with sneering sarcasm. 'I doubt it. Perhaps a little more treatment will make you more cooperative.' He nodded again to Rostov, who gave a broad grin and once again flicked the switch. Fanshaw jolted in a violent spasm but made no sound. He had passed out with the pain and the previous loss of blood.

After five hours of torture, it was now obvious to Gudenov that his prisoner did not have the information he needed. He looked at Rostov and said, 'We have no more use for him. You know where to dispose of the body.'

He then opened the cell door and walked down the long, dimly lit underground corridor until he entered the square inner courtyard of the Lubyanka. He took a deep breath of fresh air to clear the foetid stench of the prison's bowels from his nostrils. He then lit up a good Havana and inhaled long and slowly. At least Castro had offered some benefits in exchange for the millions of roubles propping up his Caribbean backwater.

'These English can be stubborn bastards,' he said to himself, then walked briskly over to his private office in the north wing, overlooking the river.

Alexei Gudenov had just passed his forty-fifth birthday but he was not concerned about the onset of middle age.

Regular exercise and a balanced diet kept him very fit. Nevertheless, he did enjoy the occasional gourmet meal, when he allowed himself a fine French claret and, to finish, a glass of cognac, which he preferred to the native Russian vodka There were certain privileges in belonging to the ruling class, the nomenklatura.

He was about 6 feet 1 inch tall, lean and erect, with blond cropped hair and blue eyes. These latter characteristics were unusual for a Russian and suggested some Germanic ancestry. When he was captured by the invading German Army led by Paulus in 1942, his features had helped him escape in the uniform of the German guard who he had throttled in the toilet a few hours before his own impending execution. He recalled the incident of twenty-five years ago with pleasure and satisfaction.

When socially relaxed, his face was handsome, open and friendly, which made him appealing – especially to women. He had a straight, rather thin nose, not at all like the wide, flat look of his Slav colleagues. His blue eyes were made to work to his advantage, reflecting his mood: hypnotic, sensuous, ice-cold or steely. At work he rarely smiled or showed emotion, unless it helped to achieve his objective. Logical analysis, sifting of information, breaking down resistance and the detection of truth and lies were the skills he had mastered over a long apprenticeship.

Clothes were also important to him. His dark blue uniform was always impeccable: no loose threads, stains or missing buttons. Simple gold-braided lapels noted his rank, and the one decoration he wore, The Order of Lenin, denoted his worth. Subordinates and equals respected him. Many feared him. Few liked him.

Gudenov did not care unduly about the opinion of people – nor needed to, while ever he enjoyed the favour and protection of the General Secretary of the Communist Party. He was good at his job, and he knew it. But this problem – finding the highly placed traitor within the very rambling Soviet bureaucracy – was proving more difficult than he had anticipated. He would need to go over the debriefing transcripts of Comrade Blake, and perhaps interview the defector again, to see if any vital clues had been overlooked. It was going to be an interesting day.

16

The Roman Connection

Joseph Demiuk was deeply religious. Since his boyhood he had always wanted to be a priest. His parents were strict Catholics belonging to the Ukrainian Catholic Church, which was in communion with Rome. Like the official Orthodox Church, it had been persecuted by the Communist regime. It operated as an underground church, bereft of any state privileges. However, provided it remained mute and powerless, the Soviet authorities ignored its existence and even allowed some churches to remain open for worship. Those who attended were mainly elderly, staunch in their faith, and they accepted the state crackdown as a necessary evil to be tolerated and passively resisted.

Joseph had been chosen by his local parish to study for the priesthood at the Ukrainian College in Rome. At the age of eighteen he had attended the Pontifical Gregorian University, which was administered by the Jesuit order, and had commenced his studies in philosophy and theology. The Ukrainian College was like a hall of residence, typical of British universities. Here he would do his private studies, participate in group tutorials and enjoy the friendship and pastimes of his fellow students. The college head and deputy were invaluable sources of guidance and advice.

He had already spent five years at the college and had two more to do before he would be ready for ordination to the priesthood.

The recent visit by his brother Bogdan had been a pleasant surprise The brothers had got on well since childhood, although Bogdan was mildly sceptical of Joseph's religious beliefs. He did not believe in God, although he respected the Church for its individuality and its opposition to the virulent atheism of the state.

The two brothers went out for an excellent meal, paid for by Bogdan, at the Tre Scallini in Piazza Navona in the heart of the ancient city. Joseph was now very familiar with the city's geography, knowing where the most famous sites were situated as well as possessing a good knowledge of bars and restaurants.

They talked about family and friends and their beloved homeland as they sat relaxing after their meal, sipping an Italian Chianti and enjoying a cigarette. Then Bogdan said to Joseph, 'I want you to do something for me.'

Joseph smiled. 'Of course,' he said, and jokingly added, 'provided it's legal.'

Bogdan laughed but ignored the latter comment from his brother.

'I want you to take this envelope to the English College, in the Via di Monserrato, and give it personally to the rector.'

'Well, that shouldn't be difficult. The college isn't too far from here. But why me? Couldn't you deliver it yourself? said Joseph.

'I'd rather not,' replied Bogdan.

Joseph pressed him. 'But why not? What does the

envelope contain?'

'I'm not at liberty to say – and the less you know, the better. However, if I tell you that the contents could have a decisive effect on the struggle between freedom and control, democracy versus dictatorship and good against evil, then you will have a general sense of what is at stake without knowing any details.'

Joseph was silent for several seconds, then nodded, saying, 'OK, but I hope it doesn't get you into any trouble.'

'No, it won't,' replied his brother. 'Also, a cleric visiting another clerical college in Rome would hardly arouse any suspicions… There are so many of you.'

'Well, no time like the present. I'll walk to the college now,' said Joseph, 'and I expect you will need to get to the airport to be in good time for your flight back to Moscow.'

'Indeed,' said Bogdan. 'I do appreciate you acting as postman for me. I'll be in touch in a week or two.'

The two brothers embraced and said their goodbyes. Joseph then made his way to the English College.

17

The Venerable English College, Rome

Monsignor James Burke was a portly man with a florid face and a balding head. He had a good sense of humour and was the ideal person to manage the students and visiting clergy who at various times stayed at the college to study or attend meetings in Rome. His appointment as Rector of the Venerabile Collegio Inglese, to give the English College its Italian title, was approved by the overwhelming majority of the English hierarchy.

Monsignor Burke had taken up his post in April 1960 after a five-year spell as director of vocations in the Diocese of Westminster. He thoroughly enjoyed his job and was well regarded by his students as well as by the many religious and secular organisations that he was involved in, due to his position as rector.

He had been surprised when the British ambassador to the Vatican had contacted Cardinal Forcellini to ask whether he would be agreeable to help the British government in a vital matter of national security. The monsignor had agreed to the cardinal's request but had been given little information about the substance of his role in this enterprise. He had only been told that he would receive a visit shortly from a reliable contact who would meet him at the Venerabile. He was to practise that most difficult of virtues: patience.

Joseph left the Piazza Navona, and his route to the English College took him through some of the most famous and beautiful parts of the Eternal City. He eventually crossed the busy Corso Vittorio Emanuele, where motor scooters zipped dangerously in and out of the heavy traffic of cars and buses. He went up through the Campo de' Fiori, which was ablaze with summer flowers, and entered the Piazza Farnese. Here he stopped briefly to admire the Palazzo Farnese, which stood on the western side of the square. Majestic and beautiful, it was a fitting edifice to house the French Embassy.

He then crossed the cobbled piazza, taking the corner road on the right, the Via di Monserrato. He passed the Bridgettine Convent on his right and soon found number 45, the address for the English College. As he entered through the open double doors he came to a desk on his right, where the college janitor greeted him. Unsure as to how his meeting with the rector would proceed, Joseph felt some apprehension.

'Good day, Father. How can I help you?' Gennaro asked in his distinctive Roman accent.

'I would like to meet the rector, Monsignor Burke, please. He should be expecting me,' said Joseph.

'Very good. Wait a moment and I will telephone him.'

Gennaro spoke to the rector, who asked him to show his visitor to his private rooms. The two men ascended the wide staircase to the third floor and were greeted by the monsignor.

'Grazie, Gennaro,' he said, and then firmly shook Joseph's

hand. 'Do you speak English?' asked the rector.

'Yes, it was a compulsory language class at school back in the Ukraine,' answered Joseph.

'Good, So, I take it that you are from the Pontifical College of St Josephat. What can I do for you?' said the monsignor as he lit up a cigarette and offered one to his guest.

Joseph put his hand in his inside pocket and pulled out a letter. 'My brother asked me to give you this letter personally. I do not know the contents, other than it is important to the British government and the interests of the West.'

The monsignor raised an eyebrow. 'And who is your brother and what does he do?'

'He is the deputy director of the Soviet space department,' said Joseph.

Hmm, thought the rector. *This gets interesting, and it suggests some sort of espionage.* He decided to press Joseph for more information.

'Do you have any knowledge at all about the contents of the letter? For instance, what is your brother's specialism in the space department and why could he not deliver the letter himself? Presumably he has recently been here in Rome to see you.'

'Yes, he has been here for a few days but has now returned to Moscow. He does not trust the KGB, who have a network of spies in every major Western country. He assumed that a priest visiting a seminary would not be judged unusual and would therefore not attract attention. All I know about his scientific background is that he collaborated with the distinguished Soviet engineer and rocketry pioneer, Vasili

Mishin. His specialty is now in space rockets. Also, I was to tell you that the letter would be collected by a young Englishman within the next couple of weeks. His name is Thomas Gillespie and he was a student here at the Venerabile in the early sixties.'

Joseph could see that the rector was having difficulty in absorbing all this information.

'My goodness,' said Monsignor Burke, 'this is fascinating information. It looks as though we are both pawns in some highly classified activity at the top of government. I'm not entirely surprised by what you have told me. A few days ago, Cardinal Forcellini, the Vatican's Secretary of State, asked me to help in a very secret liaison with the British government. I feel very uneasy about my involvement, but I assume that if Cardinal Forcellini has agreed it then it is morally acceptable. Please do not mention the cardinal's involvement in this affair to anyone, even your superior. It is obviously vitally important work, in which we are minor players.'

'Very well, Monsignor Burke,' said Joseph. 'Our conversation is safe with me. Thank you for seeing me and for looking after my brother's letter. Please God that whatever this letter contains arrives in the correct hands and that good will come from it.'

'Amen to that,' said the rector. He gave his guest a warm handshake and bade him farewell.

18

From Moscow to Yalta

The route to Yalta was taken through Kharkov, which was a medium-sized town about seventy kilometres south of Moscow. However, as they passed through the town in the dead of night, a hidden disaster almost wrecked the car. Without any warning – lights or signs – the friends nearly drove straight into a trench running diagonally across the road. Fortunately the headlights of their car gave a few moments' notice, and Bernie's skilful driving prevented them from going headlong into the trench.

'Stupid bastards.' they all shouted, followed by a further torrent of abuse towards the absent workers who had left such a dangerous and unmarked open trench on the main road. Their expressions of anger and fear were cathartic, and brought on by fatigue. Exhausted, they pulled up near a deserted field, drove through its open gate, pitched the tent and fell quickly asleep.

By 6 a.m. they were back on the road. The sun was up. It was going to be an extremely hot day. Much has been written about the freezing, snowbound Russian winters that destroyed both Napoleon's and Hitler's armies, but very little about the searing heat of the summers.

They passed through the Crimean Peninsula, unimpressed by the shallow, smelly Sea of Azov, and entered Simferopol, a holiday town that was attractive, clean and spacious. From there they climbed over the hill pass to Yalta, with Lara starting to groan but still performing admirably – so much so that they were stopped and severely cautioned by the police for speeding.

They arrived at the extensive campsite in Yalta at about 5 p.m., relieved that the car had not broken down. Now was the time to give her a long rest and some TLC. Bernie and Dunk knew the drill and what to do. Tom was useless at car maintenance and never embarrassed his friends by pretending he wasn't.

As they pitched camp, a couple of motorbikes drove slowly past, seemingly giving them the once-over. But the friends thought nothing of it and started to prepare something to eat. Bread, sausage meat, mustard, biscuits and apples – not a patch on their gourmet meals of caviar and champagne in the Moscow camp. Still, it was food. They were hungry, and a cool beer from the camp kiosk was most welcome.

'This Russian brew isn't too bad at all,' remarked Tom. 'Much better than that sewage back in London – Watney's Red Barrel.'

'Aye,' said Dunk, 'but not a patch on McEwan's Export.'

This was the start of a lively debate, typical of young men, in which there is never any agreement, about the respective merits of British and foreign beers.

Not long after finishing their frugal meal, the three friends noticed that the two motorbikes had returned. They honked their horns to get the friends' attention. They saw that one of the bikes carried a passenger – a girl. She gracefully dismounted from her pillion seat and started walking towards them. She was absolutely gorgeous.

'Hello,' she said. 'Are you English or American?' She spoke excellent English and gave a beautiful smile.

Pointing to Bernie, Tom replied, 'We are English.' Then, nodding his head towards Dunk, he added, 'and he is Scottish.'

'Well, how nice to meet you. My name is Loda. What about you?'

They all gave their names and deliberately kept quiet. This was an unusual situation. There was more to this meeting than mere chance. What did she want?

Loda then told them how much she admired the English and had been very keen to learn the language at school and college. She described her current job as a carer in a local rest home, which also served as a holiday hostel for factory workers throughout the summer. The two men who had given her a lift to the campsite also worked at the hostel.

She often asked one or other of the factory workers to bring her there because she liked to meet English speaking tourists and practise her language skills. It was fun and rewarding to spend time with people from different backgrounds. They listened with not much interest at first, as they chewed their bread and supped the local beer. However, they offered her a drink, which she readily accepted.

Beautiful but boring, Tom thought. But there was an air of mystery and expectancy about her.

It was Bernie who asked the casual but unlocking question, 'So how did you come to work down here? Are you from Yalta?'

She became serious, lost her easy smile, and started speaking slowly about her provenance and career so far.

19

Loda

She now held their interest, and their eyes could not help but admire her beauty. She was physically beautiful both in form and feature. She stood at around five and a half feet tall with slender legs, an hourglass figure, a full bosom, a narrow waist and curvaceous hips. Her dark golden hair fell past her shoulders and down her back and, when caught in the summer breeze, would gently sway like the lush, soft corn that was ripening on the Steppes. Her high cheekbones were particularly noticeable and gave her face a distinctive angular beauty.

Her clear blue, attractive eyes suggested a Germanic influence, as did her lighter complexion and smooth skin. Yet her outward appearance betrayed little of her inner state except for the occasional narrowing of her eyebrows and a sudden seriousness in her face, which was otherwise usually open and friendly.

The circumstances of her early life had been traumatic. Her biological father had been an SS officer during the invasion of the Soviet Union in Hitler's Operation Barbarossa in 1941-42. He had raped her mother, who was at that time an active member of Stalin's Young Communist League in Smolensk. He had left her for dead as the German Army had pushed on towards Moscow. She never knew nor cared what had happened to her father. She hated him. Her mother had survived and, not knowing whether the child she carried was the German's or her beloved boyfriend Grigor's, she decided to endure the pregnancy but sadly died in childbirth.

She told them she was named Loda, after her mother, and had been brought up in the local orphanage, where she was generally treated with kindness despite her obvious paternal parentage.

Though the friends were very wary of this beautiful woman, they were impressed by her life story and felt it would be unkind not to let her spend some time with them. However, they would have been surprised and alarmed if they had known more about her and her role in the Soviet Intelligence Agency.

After telling the story of her early life, Loda became suddenly very quiet, as if her history needed yet more time to be fully absorbed. It was Bernie who broke the silence.

'I think I had better start working on Lara. That sixty-six octane Russian petrol has given the engine the heebie-jeebies.'

Loda was quickly back in the conversation. 'Who is Lara?' she asked.

'Lara is our faithful old car. We named her Lara after the heroine in *Doctor Zhivago* by Boris Pasternak,' explained Bernie.

'Oh, how charming,' she replied. 'Do you have car trouble? You are so far away from England.'

'Nothing that Bernie can't fix. He's a genius with cars,' said Dunk.

'Do you mind if I watch you repair the car? I might learn

something.' said Loda.

'Not at all,' said Bernie. 'You could help by carrying some of my tools.'

'How many kilometres have you travelled in this old car? It does not look very strong.'

'We have travelled over 3,500 kilometres from central England to here. We passed through Belgium, West Germany, East Germany and Poland before arriving in your country, Russia.'

'My country is Ukraine, not Russia,' she sternly replied, and then continued in a friendly manner about how impressed she was with the journey. But her questioning soon changed to life in Britain, which seemed to be her main interest.

Bernie felt as if he was being interrogated, and at a suitable pause in their conversation said, 'The repairs have now all been done, so I need to give Lara a test run. I could take you back to your care home.'

'Oh … yes, please. That would be much appreciated.'

Bernie told Dunk and Tom that he was taking Loda back in the car and she said she would see them again tomorrow.

Night comes quickly on the Black Sea coast, so by the time they reached the top road overlooking Yalta Bay it was dark. They stopped for a brief time in a lay-by admiring the sheer beauty of the moonlight across the bay. From the harbour, far below, a yacht glided silently out to sea away from the glittering lights on the waterfront.

Suddenly, a piercing beam of light shot out from the shore, instantly focusing on the white hull of the vessel. With the yacht identified, the search light swept the rest of the bay before being extinguished. It was a stark reminder that even in attractive holiday resorts, surveillance in the USSR was not very far away.

As they continued their drive, Loda became more agitated and nervous. She would occasionally glance behind her as if expecting to be followed. She missed the correct turning to her destination and Bernie had to retrace part of the route before she was able to confirm that they were on the right road.

He was also starting to feel anxious. Was this enigmatic and beautiful girl leading him into a trap? Admittedly, she had not made a pass at him, nor he to her, but her present behaviour was completely different from their previous encounters. A roadblock installed by the KGB might suddenly appear and she could accuse him of kidnap and rape. His brain was starting to go into overdrive when, turning round a bend in the road, a large square brick building came into sight.

'This is it,' she said. 'Stop by the side door on the right. I will see you tomorrow. Thank you.' And she was gone. On the drive back to the campsite, Bernie felt very relieved. Thankfully, his fears had proved groundless, but he knew there was something strange about her. The friends had to be on their guard, or else they would land in serious trouble.

Loda had gradually become steeped in the Communist Party's ideology, and at the age of eighteen was enrolled as a trainee recruit for the secret police. Her beauty made her the ideal agent for the entrapment of gullible Westerners. She particularly enjoyed her assignments targeting West German diplomats, for her hatred of Germans was pathological. Yet she knew that her own feelings must not cloud her judgement and risk jeopardising an operation.

This she had mastered, with excellent results. High-ranking Westerners who had been photographed with her in compromising situations had yielded some valuable secrets to the state. Her employers were extremely impressed, and she had recently been congratulated by the General Secretary himself, in person. Her present assignment was going to be different, interesting and – she hoped – enjoyable.

There were three young British men heading for the Black Sea resort of Yalta in an open-topped Ford car. Her KGB controller had explained that it was assumed that one of them might have vital information about a double agent in the Soviet Defence Ministry. She was to find out for certain whether this was true and get them all arrested as foreign spies. They could then be imprisoned, with justification, for questioning.

Loda expected another success and planned her mission with meticulous care. She had worked out an entrapment plan with a difference. It was simple, and, as she packed her sexiest summer clothes, she was sure it would work. However, she knew very little about her quarry, and nothing about their briefing, background and ruthlessness.

She was in for a surprise.

20

Gudenov Becomes Suspicious

The director of the KGB had good reason to be pleased. The espionage work done by Comrade Philby and latterly by Comrade Blake had proved invaluable in keeping one step ahead of the Western powers. However, both these excellent operatives were now living in Moscow. Their information had enabled Gudenov to completely destroy both the American and the British spy networks operating within the Warsaw Pact countries. Yet he knew it would only be a matter of time before another network was put in place. Such was the nature of international espionage.

He was also acutely aware that the greatest prize known to mankind was at the centre of an uncompromising rivalry between the great powers of the United States and the Soviet Union. Who would be the first to put a man on the Moon? In 1961 President Kennedy had encouraged NASA to achieve this objective before the end of the decade. There were only three years left before the end of that timeline. He knew that Kennedy had acknowledged the superiority of the Soviet space programme and given his then vice president a blank cheque to spend on the Moon project. NASA had caught up fast and were now almost equal in the fields of science and technology to their Soviet rivals. President Lyndon Johnson was pulling out all the stops to win the race to the Moon.

In the realm of international politics the prize was huge. Whichever country was able to land a man on the Moon first would be seen by the rest of the world as the greatest power on earth. The values and lifestyle of that country would be accepted as superior to any other. There was a lot at stake.

A major part of the director's job was to make judgements concerning the likelihood of potential breaches of security. He knew that space rocketry was indispensable for a successful Moon landing. The achievements of the Soviets in the 1950s and early 1960s were spectacular. They had been the first to put a satellite, the Sputnik 1, into space, followed by the phenomenal success of enabling a man, Yuri Gagarin, to orbit the earth. The prestige and favourable publicity had been immense.

However, in recent years the Soviet space programme had encountered a number of problems and had slowed down, notably after the mistakes and inadequate research by Comrade Vasili Mishin. The role of deputy director of space rocketry had been taken by a Ukrainian, who was due a security assessment, as befitted all high-ranking officials. Gudenov asked his secretary to bring him the file of Comrade Deputy Director Bogdan Demiuk.

He reached for one of the excellent Havana cigars from a box given to him by the Cuban president, Fidel Castro. The sweet aroma of the cool smoke was a rare pleasure that he allowed himself. He then opened Demiuk's file and began reading.

Both his parents had joined the Ukranian army in the early days of the German advance in 1941. His father was an infantryman and his mother a truck driver. Both were devout Catholics and had tried to bring up their sons in the Catholic faith, despite the restrictions from the state authorities. His father was killed in the Battle of Stalingrad, but his mother survived the war and then married a Ukrainian engineer. She died of breast cancer in 1963.

Demiuk had one younger brother, Joseph, and no other siblings. Both attended school at the National Academy of Kiev and were exceptional students. Bogdan specialised in science and his brother the humanities. In 1957 Bogdan won a place at Cambridge University in England that had been negotiated by the two governments. After graduating with a first-class honours degree, he did a further two years of practical study at the Bristol-based company BAE Systems.

Demiuk returned to the USSR in June 1963 and was immediately employed in the Space Development Agency, with specific responsibility for rocket science. His knowledge and experience ensured rapid promotion to the post of deputy director in September 1965.

Gudenov paused and considered what he had read so far. Demiuk had an admirable background and curriculum vitae. His time in England could have caused a problem, but there were no reports of any suspicious activities. Moreover, many students from the Soviet Union had studied overseas and returned home as model citizens. He read on.

Demiuk married Natasha Petrovna, a childhood sweetheart he had met at the Kiev Academy. They had two children, a boy and a girl, and lived in a spacious apartment in a very desirable district of Moscow. They enjoyed holidays in Yalta, where Demiuk's position and salary had made it possible to rent a cottage with spectacular sea views.

Gudenov closed the file and considered what he had just read. One important factor that sprang to mind was that Demiuk was not a member of the Communist Party. Another was that his younger brother had been allowed to leave the Ukraine and study to be a Catholic priest in Rome. Demiuk would occasionally visit his brother and indulge in one of his favourite pastimes: Italian art and literature. Gudenov knew about these visits to Rome and raised no objection.

There was nothing else in the personal life of the deputy director that interested the head of the KGB. However, it was a ruling of the Politburo that all high-ranking officials of the state should be members of the Party. This omission could have been a clerical error when the dossier was first set up, or it could be something more significant. Nevertheless, it needed investigating. He decided to call Demiuk to a face-to-face interview.

21

The Interview

Bogdan Demiuk was not surprised that Gudenov had asked to see him. Since he had been promoted to the position of deputy space director, he knew that the paper vetting would be followed eventually by a face-to-face interview by the head of the KGB. Although Gudenov had been on the original promotion panel he had raised no questions. The other two members of the panel had been scientists.

'Good morning, Comrade Demiuk. How are you?'

'Very well, thank you, Comrade Gudenov. And you?'

'Fine,' said Gudenov, and motioned Demiuk to a comfortable armchair.

'This discussion is purely a formality,' the KGB director said. 'I see from your personnel file that you spent time in England, studying at Cambridge and Bristol Universities. Did you enjoy your time there?'

'Yes, but I missed Kiev,' replied Demiuk.

'You will be aware that in my job I have to ask specific and uncomfortable questions,' said Gudenov.

Demiuk remained silent and waited.

'Did the British MI6 ever contact you?'

'Yes, they asked me to spy for them and offered a substantial reward if I agreed, with the option of British citizenship. I refused, stating that I was a loyal citizen of the Soviet Union and was not at all interested in espionage.'

'They would have paid you handsomely. Were you not a little tempted?' asked Gudenov.

'No. My pay here is good, and I had no intention of being a traitor,' said Demiuk emphatically.

Gudenov nodded his approval. 'Your educational achievements, training and personal details are exemplary. However, there is one important omission which puzzles me.'

'And what is that, Comrade Gudenov?' asked Demiuk.

'There is no mention that you are a member of the Party.'

'True. I am not. I am a scientist, not a politician. I have no interest in politics,' answered Demiuk. 'But if you advise that I should join the Party as deputy head of space science, then I have no objection.'

'Yes, I think you should, since it is a recommendation of the Politburo that all citizens in senior state positions should be members of the Communist Party.'

'Very well, Comrade. Consider it done,' replied Demiuk.

'Excellent. I now wish to discuss an issue which greatly concerns our government, namely the progress of the Moon mission. We have reliable information from the US that NASA have made enormous strides in vital areas such as spacesuits, capsules, food, simulated landings and so on. However, they are still having problems with their rocket development. So where are we at? How long do you think it will be before we can put a man on the Moon and safely return him?'

Demiuk stroked his chin and thought for a few moments.

'All our equipment and technologies are ready. But, like the US, we have to finalise our rocket programme.

However, I am confident that we shall be ready within four years.'

'So,' said Gudenov, 'that will take us to 1971. Is it possible to bring your plans forward to attempt the mission before 1969? The General Secretary and the Politburo would be delighted if that could be achieved. However, I do not speak as a scientist, and would defer to your expert knowledge.'

'Yes, we could attempt the landing, but it would be very risky. It would endanger the lives of our cosmonauts, so it is a risk not worth taking. If we failed it would not only put our space programme back several years, but it would also bring worldwide condemnation on our scientists and – more significantly – our government.'

Gudenov nodded. 'I understand. So 1971 it is. Let us hope the Americans take longer.'

'I am sure they will. We have the advantages of the Soyuz rocket, which is progressing well after some disappointing trials.'

'Good. Well, our meeting is now finished,' said Gudenov. 'By the way, did you enjoy your trip to Rome to see your brother?'

Demiuk's face showed a flicker of surprise, but he quickly realised that very little escaped the notice of the KGB.

'Yes. It was most enjoyable, and it gave me a short time to relax from the stresses of my job.'

'Indeed,' replied the KGB director. 'It has been a pleasure to meet and talk with you, Comrade Demiuk. My very best wishes for the success of your vital space project.'

The two men shook hands and parted on friendly terms. Gudenov considered their meeting. All his answers were so perfect. Not a hair out of place. It wasn't natural. No hesitations, no uneasy body language, no nervous clearing of the throat. Nothing.

He decided to increase the surveillance on Comrade Deputy Director Demiuk to twenty-four hours a day for the foreseeable future. He had a gut feeling that something was wrong but had not a shred of evidence to substantiate this.

As Demiuk walked briskly back to his office across the bridge over the River Moskva, he considered how easy it had been for him to lie.

22

Yalta Beach

It was a scorching hot August day. Demiuk had taken his family to Yalta the previous week, not long after his 'discussion' with Gudenov. He had needed a break. Today was definitely a beach day. His wife had packed a large bag with towels, buckets and spades and an alfresco lunch of tuna and cucumber sandwiches, cake, fruit and plenty of soft drinks, with a couple of beers for her husband. Demiuk dressed the children and made sure they had plenty of suntan lotion on their face, arms and legs. It was only a short walk from their dacha to the beach, which would soon be crowded with holidaymakers from the local hotels and the workers' seaside hostels.

Tom, Bernie and Dunk had arrived early on the beach, and had established themselves near one of the cold showers positioned at regular intervals along the top side of the beach. It was blisteringly hot, and the cold showers were very welcome.

Loda had been invited the night before to join them. Her local knowledge and language skills could be very useful. She was looking ravishing in a cream bikini, with her long golden hair reaching to the middle of her back. The heads of several young men and youths turned frequently in their direction.

'It's bloody hot,' said Tom. 'I'll look around for a drinks kiosk and get some beers. What would you like, Loda?'

'An orange juice, please,' said Loda, who was already stretched out on her beach towel soaking up the sun. 'There's a kiosk over there just past the third shower. Would you like me to come with you and do the talking?'

'Don't worry,' said Tom. 'You look so comfortable lying down there, looking like a film star. I'm sure I'll be able to make myself understood. Now, what about you two ugly buggers? What would you like? Beers, I presume.' Dunk and Bernie nodded and grinned, making rude signs to their 'insulting' friend.

Tom went off on his mission and soon returned with ice-cold drinks.

'Beats Bognor,' said Bernie, with a grin.

'Bugger Bognor, as some old fart said. It even beats Blackpool and Scarborough,' said Tom as he sipped his beer and peered at a couple of scantily clad girls a few metres away.

'But not Cullen,' said Dunk. 'Hotter, yes, but it can't compete with the scenery. That beautiful bay, the golden sands – and let's not forget the golf course just past the beach. Then of course, the Anchor Pub selling one of the best pints of McEwan's in the Highlands. You know what I'm talking about, don't you, Tom?'

Tom nodded in complete agreement. 'A magical place, Dunk. A magical place.'

All four then lay back on their beach towels to soak up the sun. After about ten minutes a brightly coloured ball bounced off Tom's leg. He raised himself up on his elbow and saw a little girl standing a few metres away, smiling and pointing to the ball. She was speaking to him in Russian, which he could not understand.

'Loda,' he said, 'What is this little girl saying?'

Loda spoke a few words to her, and the little girl answered. 'Can I have my ball back, and an ice cream?' she said.

Tom burst out laughing. 'Well, well, she certainly isn't backward in coming forward,' he said, and rolled the ball back towards her. He then rummaged in his pockets for some money to buy her an ice cream.

Their new-found young friend was chatting away to Loda when a tall, muscular man came towards them. 'My apologies,' he said. 'I must have thrown the ball a little too hard for her to catch.' He pointed to his wife and son, who were sitting about twenty metres away. Loda translated, and he then spoke to them in fluent English. 'Are you American or English?' he asked.

Tom replied as he had done a few days ago when Loda had asked the same question.

'Good,' said the man. 'I spent time in England several years ago and thoroughly enjoyed it. My name is Bogdan and this is my little daughter, Natasha.' He bent down and shook hands with all of them.

'I see you have nearly finished your drinks,' said Bogdan. 'Let me buy you all another one, since I shall be going over to the kiosk to buy ice creams for my family.'

'Sure,' said Tom, intrigued by the friendliness of this stranger. He wondered to himself whether this could be the contact they were expecting.

'That's very kind of you. I'll come over with you. These lazy buggers won't budge in this heat,' joked Tom. 'Oh, I didn't mean you, Loda,' he added hastily as she gave him a quizzical look. 'I'll get you another orange juice.'

Bogdan took his little girl into his arms and went with Tom to the kiosk. When they were out of earshot from the rest, Bogdan addressed him in Italian. '*Parla italiano, signore?*' ('Do you speak Italian, sir?')

'Yes. And my name is Tom.'

At this Bogdan's eyes lit up, and from then on they spoke in Italian.

'Very good, Tom. I wonder if, like me, you have a great love of Dante.'

So this Bogdan seems to be our contact, thought Tom. But he needed more information before he could be sure. They continued speaking in Italian as they approached the kiosk, but nobody paid them any attention. It was normal to see foreign tourists in Yalta during the summer.

'Where did you learn to speak Italian?' asked Tom.

'In Rome. My brother Joseph lives there. He is studying to be a priest for the Catholic Ukrainian Church. I often go to visit him. I have also developed a passion for Italian art and literature, particularly Dante, and so it was important for me to read and speak Italian. I went to see my brother a few weeks ago. My superiors in the government are well aware of my trips to Rome and are quite relaxed about it, but not too pleased with my brother's chosen career. Also, while in Rome, I was able to hand my brother a letter that would have been difficult to post from here, where all communications from people like me are read by the KGB.'

'Are there any other favourite books that you particularly like?' asked Tom.

'Well, yes. There is a very funny English book, written

in the last century. I am sure you know it. It's *Three Men in a Boat.*'

'Yes, a great book. It's a few years since I read it, but the humour is superb. It's about time I read it again.'

They collected the drinks and ice creams. Bogdan waved to his wife, who was motioning him to get a move on.

'My wife and children are eager for their ice creams. I had better go. It was good to meet you. I hope we meet again soon someday.' He shook Tom's hand and gave him a slight nod. He then turned and headed towards his family.

Tom made his way back to his friends and Loda, convinced that Bogdan was Dante. He now knew the book needed for the code. All that was required was to collect the letter in Rome. 'Easy-peasy,' he said to himself, and grimaced. The adventure and the danger had finally begun.

23

Loda Makes Her Move

The heat of the sun started to reduce about 5 p.m., so the three friends and Loda decided to return to the campsite. On the way back, Dunk and Bernie made a detour into the town centre to stock up on provisions and to find a garage that could supply a new oil pump to replace the faulty one. Tom and Loda went on alone to the campsite.

A slight breeze now gave some freshness to the hot, sultry weather. When they reached their tent, Tom went inside to where the water had been stored away from the unrelenting sun. Loda followed him in. She had slipped on a light white dress to cover her bikini when she left the beach. Tom was still in his shorts, with no shirt. He enjoyed the sun and always took a good tan – even in the indifferent British summers. He displayed a brown torso, flecked by black hairs on his arms, chest and back.

'Would you like a drink?' asked Tom, giving Loda a quick smile.

'Yes please,' she said, 'but I would like something else too.'

'Oh, yes?' he said. 'And what is that?'

Tom was sitting on his sleeping bag, and she knelt down beside him.

'You like sex?' she said, with a little provocative smile.

'Of course,' Tom replied, looking straight at her, and gently touched her face. He had been forewarned of a likely honeytrap by Sir Richard Temple before they had left London. And this was it. He was sorely tempted but knew there would be a price to pay for his pleasure. Yet, at that moment, desire overcame reason. He didn't care. She was here, she was beautiful, and she wanted him. She took off her dress and bikini top and began to unbutton Tom's shorts.

'Oh, yes,' she exclaimed as she saw him completely naked. She took off the bottom part of her bikini and lay down beside him. But, just then, they heard the unmistakable voice of Dunk.

'Tom, I forgot my wallet,' he shouted as he approached the tent. Loda swiftly put her dress back on as Dunk poked his face through the tent flap.

'Well, well, what have we here?' he said in mock surprise.

'Dunk, you have the worst bloody timing of anyone I know,' yelled Tom, annoyed by his friend's unexpected and unwelcome return.

'So sorry, Tom,' he replied, with a knowing grin on his weather-beaten face.

'Well, get your wallet and then piss off,' said an irate Tom. Dunk was about to make another quip but, on seeing the annoyance on Tom's face, he retrieved his wallet and left with a facetious wink. But the damage was done. The moment had passed. Tom felt deflated in more senses than one.

'Sorry, Loda, I don't feel up to it at the moment. The mood has changed.'

'That's OK, another time,' she said, and gently kissed

him on the cheek. She took the glass of juice he handed to her and, casually changing the subject, asked, 'That was a very friendly man we met on the beach. Had you seen him before?'

'Never seen him before in my life,' Tom said truthfully. He was now very careful what he was going to say to this beautiful girl.

'But I heard you speak to him in a foreign language, and I don't mean English or Russian. Why was that?'

'It was Italian. We got talking in the queue, and we discovered that we both love Italian art and literature. When I answered him in Italian he was delighted. So, for a bit of light relief and fun, we both decided to speak Italian. I was also curious to see if my grasp of the language was as good as it was a few years ago.'

'And where did you learn to speak Italian?'

'In Rome. You may not believe this, but I was studying to be a priest for a short time.'

Loda laughed out loud. 'What? You, a priest? I don't believe it. You are too – how do you say? – sexy.'

'Well, thank you for the compliment, but I've yet to prove that to you.'

'So why did you leave Rome and when?' she enquired.

Tom was becoming a little irritated. Why so many questions about my past life? he wondered. But he knew the reason. However, he did not want her to realise that he knew her true purpose in befriending him and his friends.

Then, looking into her beautiful blue eyes, his expression softened, and he said, 'I left because of people like you – gorgeous, sexy girls.'

She beamed with delight but, noting Tom's annoyance,

did not ask more questions. He knew she was the honey-trap and that everything he said would be reported back to her minder. Perhaps it was fortunate after all that their afternoon of passion had been interrupted. For now it was a pleasure that existed only in his imagination, where his better judgement told him it should stay.

24

Loda's Treachery

Bernie and Dunk returned laden with essential provisions for their departure the next day to the Ukraine and their long journey back home. Loda said her goodbyes after giving a special smile to Tom and returned to her hostel. She immediately telephoned Gudenov and related the day's events, particularly the easy way in which Tom had spoken at length in Italian to a stranger on the beach.

Gudenov was quickly able to confirm that the man on the beach was Demiuk, but he knew nothing of the British man and his companions. Perhaps they were just innocent tourists. There was no proof to the contrary. Yet it seemed unusual that the deputy head of the Soviet space programme should speak in Italian to a complete stranger.

His shadowing of Demiuk had so far revealed nothing. He decided that it would be helpful to keep a closer eye on these British tourists. If they were not as innocent as they appeared, he would soon smell a rat.

He reminded Loda of the superb trap she had set for the West German businessman Hans Holderstad, two years previously, in Munich.

'Do you remember Herr Holderstad, Loda?' asked Gudenov.

'Oh, yes. How could I forget that assignment? He became

completely infatuated with me. It was easy to persuade him to return with me to Moscow. Little did he realise that he would be accused of raping me and end up in the Lubyanka prison.' She seemed to relish the unfortunate man's predicament.

Gudenov smiled as he recalled the consternation and fear of the German when he was found guilty. His face had been a picture of utter amazement and disbelief as Loda entered the witness box and calmly lied under oath that Holderstad had raped her. She had done well, very well, and had been amply rewarded by Gudenov, who had promoted her to be one of his top agents.

It had been easy to exchange the German for Comrade Novroski. The West German intelligence agency had extracted what they needed from Novroski. He deserved to live out his life in peace, back in the fatherland. He had served the state with distinction and loyalty for many years prior to his capture in Hamburg in 1962.

Gudenov thought it was unfortunate that Loda's attempt to seduce the Englishman had been unsuccessful and told her to try again. She was to offer marriage to any of them who might be interested, or at least try to persuade them to take her back to the West. If they agreed and attempted to smuggle her out of Russia, then he would have the perfect opportunity to arrest them. He would be able to apply his special skills of extracting information from them, by torture if necessary.

A self-satisfied smile lit up his face. He gave orders to commence a full surveillance operation on the three British tourists. His subordinates suspected that their master was engaged in a crucial operation involving high politics – possibly life and death – but the details eluded them.

Chapter 25

Demiuk's Dilemma

Gudenov knew from Loda's information that Demiuk had met the three British tourists on the beach in Yalta. This struck him as unusual. Yet although he had no conclusive evidence on the Deputy Space Director, he still had a gut feeling that he could not be trusted. He decided it was time to question Demiuk again and telephoned him to arrange an appointment

After the initial pleasantries, Gudenov came straight to the point. 'While you were on holiday in Yalta, you met three British men and a young Russian woman. Why was that?' asked Gudenov.

'So you have been spying on me,' said Demiuk, with noticeable irritation in his voice. 'What exactly is the point of your question?'

'You hold a very important position in the state's space development programme. It is my job, Comrade Deputy Director, to know the reason why people such as yourself make contact with total strangers, even if there is a perfectly reasonable explanation.' said Gudenov.

'As it happened, my little girl kicked her beach ball in the direction of the group you refer to and I went to retrieve it. I got into conversation with the young men and in the interests of good relations and common courtesy I bought them a drink from the local beach kiosk,' Demiuk said, by way of explanation.

'Was that all? Did any of them speak Russian?'

'No, only the woman, who had obviously made friends with them. To the others, I spoke in English – which, as you know, I speak fluently.'

'Did you speak in any other language?' queried Gudenov.

'What do you mean?' said Demiuk, with a quizzical look.

'I understand you spoke to one of the Englishmen in Italian.'

Demiuk frowned but quickly regained his composure. 'Well, well, Comrade Gudenov, your spy or spies are certainly on the ball. Yes, I spoke in Italian to one of them, who also spoke the language. As you know, I can also speak Italian, but have very little opportunity to practise it here in Russia. It was an enjoyable diversion.'

'What did you speak about – in Italian?' asked Gudenov.

'Oh, this and that. Nothing particularly serious. We touched on some books and poetry that the Englishman had recently read. His knowledge of Italy and of Italian literature were extensive.'

'Did you say who you were? And did he say what he was doing in Yalta?'

Demiuk was now becoming very annoyed. This line of questioning was becoming very intrusive and personal.

'Comrade Gudenov, I fail to see where this line of questioning is leading. You seem to exhibit some suspicion of my motives in relation to a perfectly chance encounter on a beach.'

Gudenov's face remained impassive. 'Please answer my

questions, Comrade Director.'

'Of course I didn't say anything about my position. And as far as I could tell, the British visitors were normal holidaymakers, desirous of seeing some of our beautiful country.'

The KGB director then changed his approach. 'I understand that you have two young children, a boy and a girl?'

'Yes,' answered Demiuk, 'but what has that to do with this interview?' He became animated and started to swivel the wedding ring on the ring finger of his right hand with his free left hand, which he often did when under stress.

'Nothing, at present,' said Gudenov, who held eye contact with Demiuk while noting the irritation in his replies, his fiddling with his ring and the appearance of a few spots of sweat on his forehead. 'However, it would be tragic if anything were to happen to them because of their father's actions.'

By now, the deputy space director had had enough. He stood up, pushed his chair back and faced Gudenov.

'You obviously suspect me of something but cannot say what, and you have no evidence to support your implied accusations. You then make a preposterous statement about my children and insinuate that I may be blackmailed for some fictitious crime on my part. I intend to report you to the Politburo and the General Secretary for such reckless behaviour.'

Demiuk then strode out of the room, leaving the door wide open. The head of the KGB could not help a self-satisfied smile.

'He's rattled,' Gudenov said to himself. 'My suspicions

were correct. Something is afoot – and I will surely find out soon enough.'

On the way back to his office, Demiuk felt troubled by his meeting with Gudenov. He was sure he was under suspicion and was being watched by KGB agents. What concerned him the most was the implied threat towards his beloved children. He knew that the KGB respected no moral boundaries and would do anything, and that they would commit the vilest of crimes to obtain their objectives. And, though there was no immediate danger to his children, he could not risk their safety if, in the near future, circumstances were to take a downward turn. He decided then and there what his course of action would be.

That evening he sat down to his evening meal with his wife once the children were in bed. It was time to talk.

'My darling,' he said, 'I have something very important to tell you. This afternoon I was interviewed yet again by the director of the KGB, Comrade Gudenov. He suspects me of something which he did not disclose, but I can only assume that it is connected to my position as deputy head of space research. He also made a chilling threat that our children could be harmed, in order to place pressure on me to confess to whatever he believes I am concealing. He seems to think that my chance meeting with the British holidaymakers in Yalta during our summer vacation was planned. It is a ridiculous assumption.'

Demiuk had never told his wife about his involvement with MI6. If she knew nothing she could not be threatened or blackmailed.

'Oh, Bogdan, that's terrible,' she said. 'What are you going to do? Why should the KGB wish to harm our children?' Her face was etched with alarm.

'I told Gudenov that I would report him to the Politburo and the General Secretary but he didn't seem to care. After Khrushchev, he is the most powerful man in the Soviet Union. I doubt whether even Khrushchev could sack him or discipline him unless there was clear proof of serious wrongdoing. I am sure my complaints would fall on deaf ears.'

Demiuk paused, looked at his lovely wife and said gently: 'There is only one way to ensure the safety of you and the children. You must leave the country and travel to the West.'

'But, my dear, I have my job here in Moscow, which I thoroughly enjoy. The children are settled in a very good school, and we have some good friends nearby. Also, would it not confirm Gudenov's suspicions if I and the children left? And what about you? What would you do?'

She reached across the dining table and stroked her husband's hand. She was very worried, and the strain showed.

'You can visit Joseph in Rome. If anyone asks about your trip, tell them that you haven't seen your brother-in-law for two years, and he wishes to see you and the children. I'll let him know that you are coming. From Rome you will be able to get a flight to London, where I still have contacts from my previous time there. As for me, I'll remain here for the time being and will join you when the time is right – hopefully in a month or two. We can't risk any harm to our children, and I don't trust Gudenov in the least.'

She nodded her agreement reluctantly but knew her husband was right. Perhaps he was involved in some form of espionage that she was not aware of. However, she knew that the KGB were ruthless, and she would do anything to protect her children.

'I'll book the flights for the day after tomorrow. An immediate departure would look suspicious, coming so soon after your interview with Comrade Gudenov. But you need to ring Joseph tonight.'

Demiuk kissed her gently on the cheek. 'I'm so sorry, but it is the only way. There is no other option.'

26

From Yalta to Kiev

The night before their departure, Loda came to the campsite looking distraught and tearful. She had been accused of not following the agreed procedure in dealing with two residents in the care home where she worked. She had been sacked from her job as a carer and feared that her unemployed circumstances would render her homeless. She pleaded with them to take her back to the UK. She would marry any of them if they agreed to help her.

They suspected that Loda's offer of marriage smacked of an act of desperation. With so many borders and police checks yet to come, she should have realised that she would have been recognised and taken back to Yalta. The three friends would have been arrested and put on trial for kidnapping a Russian citizen – or, worse, for espionage.

It was Bernie who spoke first saying, 'For marriage to take place there should be love. We have only known you for a few days.'

Through her tears she retorted, 'But love will come later.'

Dunk then tried to reassure her and said they would give it serious consideration and discuss the situation with her in the morning. After more tears and pleading she reluctantly left them to ponder her predicament and made her way back to the care home, where she had been allowed to stay for a few more nights.

Once she had left the campsite, they unanimously agreed that there was no way she could come back with them. They decided, therefore, to leave the campsite early, hoping to avoid a scene with Loda.

But no such luck.

Having packed everything up by 7 a.m., they drove towards the camp's exit. There, in the middle of the road, looking as beautiful as ever, was Loda.

'Why are you leaving so early? You said you would consider my offer,' she cried. Again, she pleaded with them to take her back to England. 'Please, please, I hate it here. You must take me with you.' She seemed so desperate and sincere. Yet the three friends knew it was another attempt to ensnare them.

She clung on to the side of the car as Tom tried to steer his way past her.

'No,' he said. 'We're very sorry, but we would all be caught and arrested.' He then prised her hands off the car door and accelerated. She let out a stream of abuse in English and Russian, which the friends guessed could be translated as, 'Fuck off, then. I hope you crash.'

As the car turned to join the main road the angry, lonely and lovely figure of the beautiful Loda was clearly visible, shouting and shaking her fist.

They continued in silence for several minutes. There did not seem anything to say. It was Bernie who eventually said, 'Forget her, lads. She was obviously a honeytrap and will certainly contact her KGB minder about us. Considering our mission, she is unwanted baggage – finished business. But maybe we should have been more careful...'

Since they did not wish to drive more miles than necessary, they ignored the officially approved route through Kharkov and decided to risk a shortcut to Kiev, saving about twenty-five miles. In hindsight, this diversion could have caused trouble with the authorities, but to their surprise they were not stopped by the police and arrived safely in Kiev at their destination at 4 p.m.

At the campsite, to their amazement they saw that there was a red British double-decker bus packed with students. All the girls wore multicoloured miniskirts, which was a very welcome distraction for them after driving many miles on flat, boring roads. They then dined well on tinned steak, peas, carrots, mashed potatoes and hot chocolate, not forgetting the usual long pull of vodka. The envious eyes of their fellow campers chewing on a few strands of spaghetti disturbed them not at all.

27

From Kiev to Budapest

They rose at 5 a.m., revitalised by piping hot coffee. Since they had missed the garage the previous day for refuelling, they had to drive twelve kilometres back along their route to the petrol station.

Near the Hungarian border at Lvov, the stern-faced guards waved them down but managed a grin when they saw their Russian hats. However, the grins did not last long. The friends were told to get out of the car, which was given a thorough search. All papers, maps, notebooks and reading books were confiscated. Everything had to be taken out of the boot: all the camping gear, clothes, food, tools – the lot. Even the back seat was removed for inspection. The vehicle was then driven over an underground pit and the whole of the underside was meticulously checked.

The three travellers were sure that their worst fears were being realised. As the time of their detention lengthened, they became more anxious.

'Just as we expected,' said Bernie, 'Loda has dropped us in the crap and told her KGB boss about us, no doubt lying about our relationship with her.'

The other two nodded in agreement. Dunk showed his frustration by kicking an empty plastic bottle lying in the gutter over a wall into an adjacent field, accompanied by an appropriate expletive. Tom finished the cigarette he was smoking, flicked the stub end onto the pebbled pathway leading to the guards' office and lit up a fresh cigarette.

'What a bloody mess,' he said. 'We should have stuck to the Intourist-approved route and not made this unauthorised shortcut. That's another black mark against us.' Then, with black humour, he smiled and said to his two friends, 'See you in Siberia.'

What happened next was completely unexpected. Two of the border guards walked over to them. Their guns, which were secured in holsters, were clearly visible on the right side of their waists.

'This is it ,' muttered Dunk. 'The bastards are going to arrest us.'

However, one of the guards handed back all their documents, books and notebooks. The other had one of Dunk's books in his hand and said in faltering English, 'I learn English ... and keep this book, please?'

'Yes. Certainly,' answered a puzzled but relieved Dunk. The book was *Whisky Galore* by Compton Mackenzie. 'You will enjoy it,' he said. 'It's a good read and very funny.'

'Thank you,' said the guard. 'All of you can now go.'

The friends were dumbfounded, having expected the worst, but lost no time in repacking the boot and the back seat. They drove away from the border post as fast as the old Ford could go over a bridge into Hungary. They were amazed at their good fortune.

Once again there was the usual delay at the Hungarian border while all their documents and equipment were checked. Since they had to put their watches back by two hours, from 3 p.m. to 1 p.m., to synchronise with the new time zone, they anticipated making good time to Budapest.

No such luck. They stopped for refuelling around 8 p.m., and shortly afterwards had fish soup and goulash at a roadside restaurant. The fish to make the soup were still alive, swimming in a tank. The customer would point to a fish which the waiter would catch and then make the soup with it. Very novel, but a bit creepy.

When they were about fifteen kilometres from Budapest they were flagged down by the police, then told to drive into a lay-by and switch off their car lights. In total darkness they witnessed about 100 military trucks and a missile carrier heading towards the Russian border. This delay made them bad-tempered with each other, for no specific reason other than fatigue and frustration.

But eventually they arrived in Budapest and found the campsite on the north side of the city. They were told the site was full at reception but ignored this information when they spotted a decent plot of grass next to another car. They pitched their tent, had something to eat and drink, and crawled into their sleeping bags utterly exhausted.

The next day, after a leisurely breakfast of Hungarian chocolate, milk, rolls and Russian jam, they left the site at 10.30 a.m. and headed for the Austrian border. It was striking to see the improvement in the quality of the houses, road surfaces and consumer goods available in West Hungary in comparison with the Soviet Union. They drove alongside the magnificent Danube for several miles and at last arrived at the border post. Here, after a cursory inspection by some very affable customs men, they were waved through into Austria.

The friends breathed a great sigh of relief. They had

made it back to the West unharmed and as they presumed, undetected. So far, so good.

28

Decisions in Vienna

As they drove towards Vienna through the open countryside, the traffic started to increase, petrol stations were numerous and advertising boards were everywhere. What a contrast from the last few weeks. After buying a guidebook from a local kiosk they made their way to the camping site Wien Ost, which was set in attractive surroundings near a lake.

A fellow Austrian camper and his wife advised them that a restaurant, aptly named the Vienna Woods, in Grinzing, provided excellent meals. They took their advice and were not disappointed. The inside dining area was preceded by an open square filled with tables and surrounded by trees. They were met by the head waiter who showed them to a corner table. The inside was typically Austrian, with murals depicting local scenes, and bright lamps on the wooden alcove tables.

'We had better consider our next moves,' said Dunk as they filled their glasses with the excellent Riesling sitting in a glass carafe in the middle of the table.

'Well,' said Bernie, 'Tom is the churchy guy, and he needs to pick up that letter in Rome from the priest at the English College. Also, remember before we left London, Sir Richard told us to visit the embassy here, to collect more money and instructions.'

Tom lit up a cigarette, inhaled deeply and exhaled the smoke. 'OK. Tomorrow we shall go to the embassy, and the day after I shall leave for Rome. Then you two can leg it back to London. Apologies for mixing my metaphors, but you know what I mean – you drive like shit to Calais.

'I am sure the KGB must be on to us by now, particularly after debriefing Loda. The split, with me going south and you two north, will be a diversion and a confusion for any agents who may be following us.'

Dunk nodded. 'I agree. All three of us have half the information, because we know the title of the book. The crucial other half will be contained in the letter in Rome. So, Tom, it will be up to you to collect this letter and return with it safely to London. It's risky. But we all knew this from the beginning. Perhaps the embassy may provide some item of protection. Incidentally, Tom, you never fully explained why you were expelled from the college back in 1963. Had you been a naughty boy?'

Tom inhaled on his cigarette and told his friends what had happened. 'Yes, you could say that. You may be aware that Catholic priests are expected to be celibate. So no sex of either kind, male or female. Most of the students that I met at the college were heterosexual, but there were also those who batted for the other side within our community. Anyway, when staying at the college in Rome we were expected to go out for walks into the city every afternoon.

'I got to know Rome better than any other city – its bars, shops, piazzas and shortcuts. There was a large department store on one of the main shopping thoroughfares called Standa, similar to our Woolworths, selling all sorts of stuff.

As students we would often go there to stock up on such things as toothpaste, stationery, and similar small items – prices were very reasonable. The shop assistants were mainly young, attractive girls, some of them obviously very intrigued to see young foreign men in their clerical garb shopping for this and that.

'A family friend back in England had asked me to buy a statue of the then pope, 'Johnny Roncers' – Pope John XXIII to you. So, I asked one of the beautiful assistants in my faltering Italian if Standa had any of these statues in stock.

'She burst out laughing and said, *"Scusi, padre?"* (Excuse me, Father?) My Italian had obviously caused hilarity and obvious confusion. (When I related my Italian request to a friend and excellent Italian speaker, he also laughed out loud. Apparently, my poor Italian had asked not for a statue of the pope but for his bra.) As best I could, I rephrased my request which she understood before saying, *'No, mi dispiace'* (No, I am sorry.)

'I smiled, thanked her and said my *'ciao'*, which she acknowledged with a gorgeous smile, and then I left the shop. But I was smitten and returned every day for a week to Standa just to see her and ask her for things I did not really need to buy. We got chatting and she would gently correct my imperfect Italian, but we managed to converse well enough.

'As you can imagine, one thing led to another, and I asked her out on a date. She readily agreed. We used to meet up on her day off, when I would skip lectures and spend most of the morning and afternoon with her. But I knew I was playing with fire and that it was only a matter of time before our dalliance was discovered.

'Sure enough, I was called by the rector for a 'chat,' which turned out to be a serious bollocking. It had come to his notice – i.e. somebody had seen me with the girl and had contacted the rector – that I had been fraternising with a girl from Standa. "Is this true?" he asked. Obviously I could not deny it. So I was duly expelled from the college, as not suitable as a candidate for the priesthood.'

'Did that upset you?' asked Bernie.

'Not a bit,' said Tom. 'In fact I was relieved, since I was able to begin living a more honest life, without the pressure I had felt from my parents and the parish. Anyway, enough about me. Let's enjoy this excellent wine and meal before we return to the campsite and hopefully a good night's sleep.'

They rose at 8 a.m. Dunk and Tom went for a swim in the cool lake while Bernie prepared breakfast. They then went into the capital, parked the car near the fish market and walked towards the centre.

Vienna is a beautiful city. The boulevards are spacious, well-proportioned and stylish. And the Viennese are courteous and elegantly dressed. They asked a smart middle-aged woman for directions to the British Embassy in Jauresgasse, which she was able to give them in understandable English.

What would the ambassador say to the three friends? How much did he know about their mission? And were there more instructions from London?

They would soon find out.

29

At the British Embassy in Vienna

Sir James Sanderson was a career diplomat who was coming to the end of his service. He had spent many years in South America and had expected to see out his time there, yet to his surprise he had been given one last posting – to Vienna. But though it had been a surprise, it was a very welcome one. He spoke fluent German, and both he and his wife enjoyed holidays in the Austrian mountains, where he was able to relax completely from the pressures of his job.

He had received a telephone call earlier in the week from the British Foreign Secretary himself, informing him that a parcel and a top-secret letter would be included in the next diplomatic bag. And that three young British men would visit the embassy to collect the parcel and the letter. Nothing else was disclosed.

Sir James was discreet and obedient but could not help wondering what the parcel, the letter and the meeting with three strangers could possibly mean. However, he knew that embassies were used for security reasons, and that the specific instructions from the Foreign Secretary were most likely to have been initiated by MI6.

The following day the ambassador examined the diplomatic bag, and as expected found a parcel and a letter both addressed to a Mr T. Gillespie and wax-sealed with the stamp of the Foreign Office. Later that day, he was informed that three young British men had arrived and had asked to meet him. His secretary met the friends in the spacious foyer and led them up a magnificent staircase to the next floor. They were then ushered in through a large oak door, and saw a tall, slim and immaculately dressed middle-aged man sitting behind a large desk. He got up and said,

'Welcome, gentlemen. My name is James Sanderson,' and shook their hands. He then continued, 'I spoke to the Foreign Secretary two days ago, who said you would be coming to see me. He didn't elaborate on the reason for your visit, but asked me to hand over this parcel and this confidential letter to Mr Thomas Gillespie.'

'Yes, that's me,' said Tom, and stepped forward to receive the items.

'Just a minute, young man,' said the ambassador. 'I need to verify your identity. I also received a confidential letter containing your photograph and several personal details. So, could you please tell me, what your date of birth is?'

'It's 24 March 1943,' answered Tom.

'And what is your mother's maiden name?'

'Mary Cronan.'

'And your father's second Christian name?'

'Patrick.'

'And finally, what is your favourite football team?'

'Sheffield Wednesday.'

The ambassador smiled. 'Good. You have answered all those questions correctly and your appearance matches your photograph, although you now look slimmer and fitter.'

Sir James handed the parcel and letter to Tom and said,

'I have no idea what these contain and can only guess that the three of you are connected with our security services. But the less I know, the better. However, I was told that you would know the name of a book, and that the title should be written down on embassy notepaper, sealed in a plain envelope and simply inscribed, *Foreign Secretary: Top Secret.*'

He provided the paper, envelope and embassy seal, and then turned his back and walked towards the window. Bernie went to the desk and wrote, *Three Men in a Boat*, then inscribed and sealed the envelope.

'All done,' said Bernie.

Sir James turned round to face them. 'Then I bid you gentlemen good day and wish you success in this enterprise, whatever it is.'

The three friends thanked the ambassador and left. They needed a secluded, private place to open the parcel and so they went to a nearby park. They chose an isolated bench, away from the few parents and their children who were enjoying the swings, slides, seesaws and the other play equipment in the local play area.

The parcel contained three automatic handguns capable of firing six bullets. And three gun holsters, each containing a replacement magazine.

'Bloody hell,' said Dunk in a low voice. 'Looks like we could be in for some fun and games.' From his previous knowledge acquired at the Highland Shooting Club, he immediately recognised the type of gun and explained to his friends how to fire and reload them. 'Let's hope we don't have to use them, but they are a welcome reassurance in case they are needed.'

They each took a gun and holster and slipped them into a backpack that Dunk had brought along. But the weapons needed to be secured and hidden on their shoulders, so light casual jackets would need to be worn. The next few days could be dangerous and deadly.

30

The German Connection

At fifty-six Heinrich Mueller was at the top of his career as head of the East German security service. As a young man in 1943 he had entered the ranks of the Gestapo under the authority of Reich Führer Himmler. He adored Adolf Hitler and was fully committed to the German leader's goals of a supreme master race and expansion to gain living space for the German people in the east.

The stabilising of the currency in the early years of Hitler's chancellorship, the reduction of unemployment and the steady growth of the economy were resounding successes that proved to Mueller and millions of others that the Führer was a great leader. When Hitler survived the bomb plot on his life in July 1944, Mueller was convinced that Germany would win the war or at the very least survive it with an honourable settlement.

As a Gestapo officer he became an avid and diligent agent for the success of the Third Reich. The suicide of Hitler in 1945 (and of many other top Nazi leaders as the war in Europe came to an end) was a great shock to him. The war had been lost, but he needed to survive.

Mueller considered the Allied bombing of Dresden and of other defenceless German cities as a war crime. His older brother, Kurt, was killed when that great ship, the

Bismarck, was damaged by British naval power in 1941. His younger brother, Wilhelm, was shot by the Americans in Normandy during the D-Day landings in June 1944. He hated the British and the Americans for the deaths of his brothers and the indiscriminate and needless destruction of much of his homeland during the latter stages of the war.

He was captured by the invading Soviet Army in April 1945 while trying to escape from his Gestapo base in Leipzig. At first he was selected to be shot by firing squad the morning after his capture. However, when the Soviet authorities discovered that he was a former Gestapo agent, he was temporarily reprieved until his assessment by the KGB.

Mueller's knowledge and skills were recognised by his captors as potentially very useful in post-war Europe. His execution was duly postponed, and he was ordered to report to a KGB official who had accompanied the invading Soviet army. He recognised that with the death of his beloved Führer and defeat in war, the belief in a powerful and dominant Germany had gone forever. He knew he could work with the Russians but not the hated Western Allies, who had killed members of his family. Also, the principles and practices underpinning Hitler's National Socialism were similar to those that formed the basis for Soviet socialism.

After an intense interrogation and a six-month period of probation, he was given a post in the East German security service on its formation. With its proximity to West Germany, the country also became an important member of the Warsaw Pact. As an accomplished linguist in English and French, and possessing a range of security techniques,

Mueller soon began to be noticed by his superiors. His promotion was rapid, culminating in attaining the top job within the East German security service in the summer of 1965.

He was not surprised when Gudenov telephoned him from Moscow. They spoke regularly every month to update each other on the latest security issues and potential flashpoints.

'Good morning, Heinrich,' said the KGB director. 'I need your help.'

'Certainly,' said Mueller. 'What can I do for you?'

Gudenov explained to his counterpart what had happened in Russia and the meeting Demiuk had in Yalta with the three British tourists. His suspicions concerning the deputy space director were outlined, and they concluded in his confiding in Mueller that Demiuk could not be trusted. He continued by saying that he was convinced that the three Britons were complicit in a serious espionage plot and needed to be dealt with.

'These three British tourists have now left Hungary,' he said to Mueller. 'According to my intelligence sources they have reached Vienna and were staying in a campsite near Grinzing. I want all three to be eliminated. It is the only way to ensure that any secrets they received from Demiuk will not reach Richard Temple in London. I know I can rely on you to be thorough and discreet. We do not wish to attract unwanted publicity.'

'Very well,' said Mueller. 'I have just the men to accomplish this task. They work efficiently and stealthily, and they both speak English. Leave it with me, Comrade Gudenov. They are as good as dead.'

'Thank you, Heinrich. Your services will not go unrewarded.'

Gudenov inhaled his cigarette slowly and deeply. It was time to share this unwelcome news with the General Secretary. He did not much care for this task.

Mueller knew that he needed his most ruthless and efficient operators. He picked up the telephone and told his private secretary to contact Hans Lassis and Kurt Neuerbach. These two would finish the job without attracting undue attention.

He did not have to wait long for a response.

'Lassis here, Herr Director.'

'Thank you for your timely response, Hans. I need you and Kurt Neuerbach to do a special job on three British tourists – two Englishmen and a Scotsman. They are currently at a camping site at Grinzing in Vienna. I want them followed and then disposed of at a suitable time and place.'

He then gave a brief account of what Gudenov had told him earlier, with descriptions of the three men.

Neuerbach telephoned him within the hour. Mueller briefed him as he had Lassis, and arranged to meet both agents in his office at 6 p.m.

31

From Vienna to Rome

Tom said goodbye to Dunk and Bernie outside Vienna Railway Station and made his way to Platform 3. The express was due to depart in forty minutes' time to Rome.

He stopped at a coffee bar on the way and ordered a cappuccino and one of the excellent Viennese pastries that had become a firm favourite during the last couple of days. Near the counter was a news stand selling Austrian and foreign papers. He saw some copies of *The Times* and bought one. The front page was dominated by the economic difficulties of Harold Wilson's Labour government. There was also a lengthy article on the possibility of a manned Moon landing by the US, which the presidential candidates for the next year's election were exploiting to the full.

Tom gave a wry smile and then turned to the sports page to see how his favourite football teams were doing. Sheffield Wednesday were steadily moving up the league after a convincing away win. 'Now that's more like it,' he said to himself with a satisfying smile.

After finishing his breakfast snack Tom boarded the train, which had now arrived in the station from Berlin. There were still a good ten minutes or so before leaving, so he had plenty of time to find a comfortable window seat in a six-seater carriage not far from the buffet car. He settled down to read *The Times*. The only other person in the compartment was an attractive girl with straight blonde hair and blue eyes.

A German lass, Tom said to himself. His assessment was confirmed when he noticed the magazine she was reading, which was *Bild*. Their eyes met briefly, and Tom smiled. She smiled back and then continued reading her magazine.

The train departed on time at 7.45 a.m. A few minutes after the station's outbuildings had been left behind, the compartment's sliding door was suddenly pulled open and a well-dressed man in a grey suit carrying a black briefcase asked in German if the empty seats were taken or reserved. It was Hans Lassis. His East German partner, Kurt Neuerbach, had taken a seat in a nearby compartment to be distant from his colleague but near enough if needed.

'Nein,' said the blonde girl.

'Ah. Gut,' said the man, and sat in an empty seat away from the girl but on the opposite side to Tom, although not directly opposite him. The man attempted to engage Tom in conversation, but Tom shrugged his shoulders and said, 'Ich nich sprecken Deutsch.' (I do not speak German.) That was just about the extent of his German, so he hoped that the man wouldn't ask him anything else.

'Are you English?' the newcomer asked, in English.

'Yes,' Tom replied slowly, wary that this chap might turn out to be a crashing bore who wanted to improve his English language skills by speaking to him.

'OK. Good. But I speak not so much English, so we will have to read.' He had obviously seen Tom's newspaper. He then took out a copy of a German paper and settled down to read it.

Thank God for that, thought Tom. He was not in the mood to engage in polite, stilted conversation with a complete stranger.

Once out of the city, the train soon picked up speed. After the early start that morning, Tom started to feel drowsy and decided to have a doze. He rested his head on the cushioned seat and relaxed his body into a comfortable position. He felt the gun in the shoulder holster and was reassured. He had never had anything to do with firearms in the past, but these present circumstances were different. Even if he did not have to use the gun, it was a welcome insurance in an emergency.

The other two passengers in the compartment continued to read their papers. At one point, the man in the suit looked at Tom over the top of his paper for several seconds before continuing to read. Tom was soon asleep and his breathing was heavy, interspersed with an occasional grunt.

Tom woke with a jolt as the train entered a tunnel and gave the long, howling hoot so common to speeding trains. The lights of the compartment came on but were not needed for long, as the express soon re-emerged into sunlight.

By now it was mid afternoon. Having missed lunch, he decided to make his way to the restaurant carriage and have an early meal before the rush started around 5 p.m. The menu was varied but simple – soup, a main course, dessert, with wine, beer or a soft drink. Tom decided on lasagne and mushrooms with a glass of Chianti and a small bottle of sparkling S. Pellegrino mineral water followed by fruit salad. He then noticed, a few tables away, the German who was in their compartment. Tom nodded to him and received a nod back. 'Seems a friendly bloke,' he said to himself.

The train passed through Austria, stopping only once at a small station before crossing the Italian border on its way to Venice. Here, at the border, the train was due to stop for twenty minutes to take on customs officers, some small items of freight, and mail.

Tom decided to stretch his legs on the platform, to walk off some of his meal and have a cigarette. He bought an evening paper at a nearby kiosk and a bottle of beer for the latter part of the journey. As he turned and started to walk back to his carriage, he saw the German from his compartment also on the platform, but none of the others.

He must fancy me, he said to himself. But a more ominous thought was starting to form in his suspicious mind.

Once he was back in his seat, Tom opened his paper and read the headline about the Italian political scene: Government about to fall for the second time this year.

So what? thought Tom. That's just typical Roman politics. But another article on the second page caught his attention: *American Moon preparations stall.* There was little information other than some technical jargon about lift-off strategies.

Yet Tom knew exactly what that meant. He felt a shiver of fear, knowing what he and his two friends were expected to accomplish.

32

Arrival in Rome

From the border the train made good progress to Milan. Here many passengers left the train and were greeted loudly by family and friends, who were obviously delighted to see them. More passengers got on, including a very vocal group of about six Inter Milan supporters who were in high spirits after their team had just beaten Lazio by two goals to nil.

Always interested in talking football, Tom soon found himself engaged in a lively conversation about the top European clubs likely to feature in this season's European Champions Cup. Sadly, his own favourite club, Sheffield Wednesday, was unlikely to join the elite ranks of British clubs, such as Manchester United or Celtic, who competed at the top level. The name of Sheffield Wednesday only drew blank faces and raised eyebrows from his Italian audience.

After a very enjoyable discussion and some banter with the Inter fans, Tom returned to his compartment and decided to take a nap. He nodded to the friendly German with the briefcase, smiled at the blonde girl, who had now finished her magazine and was reading a book, and leant his head against the upholstered cushioning of his seat. He was soon dozing peacefully then fell sound asleep.

He had a weird dream. He was back in the Highlands, fishing on the River Deveron, just outside Huntly Golf

Course, with Dunk. He felt a bite on his line and hooked a big fish. He was sure it would be a fair-sized salmon, but in fact it was a pike.

Then, instead of Dunk helping with his net to land the fish on the riverbank, Dunk took out his gun, which he had collected at the Austrian Embassy, and shot the pike several times. The water started to turn red, and Tom suddenly woke from his disturbing dream. He shook his head to banish his nightmare but he felt disturbed, as if he had experienced a bad omen.

'Roma,' said the German, seeing that Tom was a little disorientated after his sleep. Tom nodded his thanks and looked out of the carriage window to see factories and high-rise blocks of flats bordering the track.

'Well, I never thought that I should be back in the Eternal City so soon after the last time,' said Tom to himself, and then stood up to take down his backpack from the luggage rack.

On arrival in the station's terminus, Tom made his way to the taxi rank and got into the back of the nearest available taxi. 'Where do you want to go?' asked the driver.

'Piazza Farnese,' said Tom. He also noted that the German passenger from his compartment had also hailed a taxi. *Hmm, interesting*, thought Tom. *I wonder if he is following me.*

The traffic was light, so it did not take too long to reach his destination. Tom walked past the corner bar and into a nearby side street to see if his hunch would prove correct. He lit a cigarette and waited.

33

Back Again to the English College

He did not have to wait long. A taxi arrived in the piazza and out stepped the German. He started to walk around the piazza and stopped briefly at each adjoining street. He was obviously searching for Tom. He also peered into the bar on the corner and the restaurant near to the French Embassy. Both these premises were now shut due to the late hour. After finding no trace of his quarry the German returned to the taxi, which then left the piazza.

Tom heaved a sigh of relief. He had given his pursuer the slip. He then made his way down the Via di Monserrato towards the English College. He was soon at number 45 and banged on the large wooden door. There was no response, just silence. He banged again, this time louder. After a few more minutes waiting a light suddenly went on and a voice enquired, '*Chi è?*' (Who is it?)

Tom immediately recognised the voice of the college caretaker, Gennaro, and replied in Italian, 'It is Tom Gillespie. I used to be a student here six years ago. Perhaps, Gennaro, you may remember me.'

'How could I forget you, Signor Tom? You liked the signorine and were sent back home. The gossip about you lasted years.'

'OK, Gennaro, OK. I wasn't exactly a model student.

However, I am here to see Monsignor Burke, the rector. Is he available?'

'But, Signor Tom, you must have forgotten that the college has moved to the villa at Palazzola for the summer.'

'Oh, bugger,' said Tom.' I should have remembered that. Since it is now late, Gennaro, can I stay here the night? I will then go to the villa tomorrow.'

'Yes, Signor Tom, but you will have to leave in the morning.'

'Many thanks. I promise to leave by 9 a.m. prompt.'

Gennaro opened the door and let Tom into the ground floor corridor of the college. They shook hands. Then Gennaro said, 'You may as well stay in your former room on the third floor. It is unoccupied at the moment, but it will be needed at the weekend.'

Tom thanked the caretaker and made his way up the wide stone staircase to the third floor.

As he climbed the stairs, Tom thought about some of the students he remembered from his past days, particularly some of the strange nicknames given to them by other groups of students or one of the prima donna characters that all institutions have. He recalled Spam, Ichabod, Trog, Hobbit, Spike, and then some of the more obvious ones: Jock, Nobby and Shirley. He wondered what they were all doing now. Hopefully, most would have been ordained priests, but not necessarily so.

He soon found his old room, which looked remarkably different from when he last occupied it. It was now an en suite with a shower, a modern single bed, soundproofed windows, a telephone on the desk adjacent to the bed, and it had been recently decorated. *Blimey,* thought Tom. *What a difference a few years can make to intelligent living.*

He undressed, had a quick shower and got into bed. He was sound asleep in minutes.

The telephone rang at 7.30 a.m.

'Buongiorno, Signor Tom,' said the cheery voice of Gennaro. 'Breakfast is ready for you down here. We have coffee, rolls, butter, cheese and apricot jam. Unfortunately, the full English is not a dish we serve in Italy.'

'Many thanks,' Tom said. 'I shall have to make do with a second-rate Italian breakfast,' and he gave a mocking but friendly laugh to his generous host.

He put his belongings into his backpack and made his way to the caretaker's rooms. After a mug of excellent coffee and an apricot jam roll, he thanked Gennaro for his hospitality and entered the Via di Monserrato.

His next destination was the villa at Palazzola on the Via dei Laghi, several miles north-east of Rome.

34

Hans Discovers the Trail

Although Hans did not see Tom in the Piazza Farnese, he was sure he must be in the area. He told the taxi driver to drive the short distance to the nearby Campo de' Fiori and then turn swiftly around and return to the Piazza Farnese.

He was just in time to see Tom turning into the Via di Monserrato. He told the taxi driver to follow Tom, but at a discreet distance. They saw Tom walk quickly past the Bridgettine Convent on the corner, but he did not look back or quicken his step. Hans was sure that he was completely unaware that he was being followed.

Tom then abruptly stopped and hammered on a sturdy large wooden door. The taxi slowed down to a crawling pace about fifty metres from the building. The door eventually opened, and Tom went inside. Hans then saw the door being firmly shut and heard the inner bolts rattle into place. As he was slowly driven past the building, he saw the nameplate: *Venerabile Collegio Inglese*. 'Gut,' said Hans and then told the taxi driver to take him to his hotel. He was sure that his quarry would not be going anywhere till morning.

At 6.30 a.m. Hans was back on the Via di Monserrato and took a window seat in a nearby cafe, from which he could see the main door of the English College. This time he had his colleague Kurt with him. They both sipped piping hot cafe lattes and munched on chocolate brioches while one of them kept the door in his sights and the other glanced through the morning paper. After about two tedious hours, Hans nudged Kurt.

'He is just leaving the college,' Hans said. They rose quickly, paid their bill and went out into the street, keeping 100 metres or so from the unsuspecting Tom. They followed him back to the Corso Emanuele Secondo and were able to get on the same tram as Tom. At the terminus, they followed him to the nearby bus station and saw him in the queue for Albano and the Via dei Laghi.

'I think we should now separate,' said Hans to Kurt. 'He may have seen us both on the tram. It could arouse his suspicions if he also sees the two of us on the same bus as him.'

'You are right, Hans,' said Kurt. 'I will get on the bus, since he will not have seen much of me on the train, but you were in the compartment with him. Where he is going is a mystery. I should have a clearer idea once he gets off the bus. You should now report back to Mueller, my friend, and tell him that we have our man fully covered. It will be impossible for him to evade our surveillance.' The two agents agreed on their action and Kurt joined the small queue for the bus to Albano. Hans telephoned Mueller from the bus station.

On the main road opposite the long lane down towards the Villa Palazzola, Tom got off the bus, crossed the road and walked down the lane towards the villa. Kurt was able to see him turn into the lane, but Tom was then out of his sight. Kurt decided to alight at the next stop, a local trattoria only about another fifty metres on. He then ran swiftly back to the lane just in time to see Tom reach a side door leading into the villa. He decided to sit under a sheltered tree until nightfall, but first he must contact Mueller with this vital information. His boss was very pleased with the news and complimented both his agents.

Mueller then rang Gudenov in Moscow, who thanked him for the diligence of his agents in their keeping his prey under surveillance from Vienna to Rome and subsequently to Palazzola. He had earlier asked Mueller to provide two more agents to eliminate the remaining two British tourists who had remained in Vienna and who had continued their journey to one of the Channel ports.

The East German spymaster reassured Gudenov that he would ensure that agents would be provided and the task successfully completed. Gudenov was pleased, and thanked his counterpart for his excellent service.

'You and your team have done an excellent job keeping surveillance over them from Vienna to Palazzola. It is now time for me to contact our Italian friends and their espionage organiser, Franco Pasolini. Many thanks for your assistance. I will not forget it.'

Gudenov then rang Pasolini.

'Ciao, Franco. I need your help to dispose of an English agent who is posing as a tourist. He is currently staying at the English villa at Palazzola, north of Rome, and being monitored by one of Heinrich Mueller's men. I would be grateful if you could supply one of your agents to take over from Mueller's man and finish the job.'

'That will not be a problem. I have just the man. Leave it with me, Alexei' said Pasolini.

'Grazie mille (Many thanks),' said Gudenov. 'I know you will not let me down.'

Pasolini then telephoned Giacomo.

'Buongiorno (Good day), Giacomo. I have a job for you.' He gave a brief description of the facts that had been explained to him by Gudenov. Having spoken to Mueller, he was able to give a description of Kurt Neuerbach.

'You are to meet Neuerbach at a nearby taverna. He will update you about the time he has been keeping watch on the Englishman, whose name is Tom Gillespie. Make sure you are in place by 6 a.m. tomorrow morning and keep me informed of your progress.'

'Certamente (Of course), Signor Franco. You can rely on me,' said Giacomo.

'Benissimo (Very well),' replied Pasolini, then finished the call.

Tom stepped into the sultry warmth of a hot Roman day from the coolness of the English College and made his way to the Corso Vittorio Emanuele. Rather than call a taxi, he decided to go by tram to the main bus station to catch the connection to Albano and the Villa Palazzola.

After an hour and a half he was dropped off at the long driveway leading down to the villa. It would be a joy to see the place again after several years. The views overlooking Lake Albano, the scented gardens, the blue butterflies, the nine-hole golf course and the swimming pool gave the villa a unique charm, perfect for rest and relaxation for stressed-out students and clergy.

It was common to see a bishop relaxing on a lounger beside the pool enjoying a cigarette and a glass of wine, the cares of his diocese in England left far behind. Boisterous students would race one another up and down the pool, occasionally splashing His Lordship, who merely smiled, perhaps remembering his own student days at the villa after a gruelling year at the Pontifical Gregorian University in Rome.

After a leisurely walk down the lane he passed the caretaker's house and the main chapel before entering by a side door, which led onto a small quadrangle with a fountain. He saw Monsignor James Burke walking slowly round the perimeter reading his breviary.

'Good day, Monsignor Burke,' said Tom.

The rector stopped and looked at Tom. 'Ah, Mr Gillespie. I have been expecting you.'

35

Giacomo Beronni

Giacomo was a killer. He had no feelings for his victims, no pity. They were dispatched with the ruthlessness of a lion killing its prey to feed its young cubs. One could say that he was a psychopath. He was not normal, as most people understand normality.

Yet his outward appearance and actions betrayed nothing of his mental condition. He lived a quiet life with his elderly widowed mother (his father had died ten years earlier). He enjoyed meeting a few friends in a local bar in the picturesque village where he lived in the beautiful countryside of Umbria. There he played cards and sampled the various local wines from nearby vineyards.

He was not around in the 1920s when Benito Mussolini came to power. However, as a teenager in 1940, he became a fascist and joined the blackshirts of Dino Grandi. He greatly admired Mussolini – Il Duce – and became one of his personal bodyguards. But events did not develop as he had hoped. Mussolini was captured by the Italian resistance and, with his unfortunate lover, was executed and their bodies hung head down, to exaggerate the revulsion that his enemies felt towards their former dictator.

Considering such events and the changed political landscape after the victory of the Allies in the war, Giacomo thought it prudent to keep a low profile, and returned to his village to consider his options. The Soviet Union now controlled the whole of Eastern Europe and was an acknowledged superpower.

Giacomo was convinced that the Russian leadership under Stalin would not be satisfied with their present geographical gains but would consider further advances into Western Europe a realistic military option. He considered that Soviet hegemony over the whole of the European continent was a foregone conclusion. He therefore joined the Italian Communist Party and became a model member, doing anything that was asked of him. Many of these tasks were in the murkier side of political intrigues.

The call from his boss, Franco Pasolini, was very welcome. Recently it had been a very quiet time. He craved action and now he had it. He had to eliminate an English tourist who was also a spy.

Pasolini explained his mission and his journey to Palazzola, where he would take over from the East German, Neuerbach.

He kissed his mother goodbye, assuring her he would be back in a week or so, and left the village in his blue Citroën. He knew Albano and the Castelli region, which was very famous for its natural beauty and superb wines.

By midnight he had arrived at the taverna near Palazzola and had no difficulty in recognising Kurt Neuerbach. They shook hands and exchanged pleasantries. Over a glass of Frascati wine Kurt fully briefed his Italian counterpart. He then returned to Rome after telephoning Mueller of the successful handover.

Giacomo dozed fitfully in the back seat of his car, then

at 5.45 a.m. he made his way to the hiding place vacated by Kurt, lit a cigarette and waited.

It was another two and a half hours before anything happened. He saw a car coming up the long lane from the villa. As it reached the top of the lane and turned onto the main road Giacomo saw that there were three people in the car: a male driver, a woman in the passenger seat and a man in the back seat. He immediately recognised that the back seat passenger was Tom.

'So the journey begins,' he said to himself. 'Excellent. My boredom will be relieved.'

36

Plans made at Palazzola

Tom shook the rector's hand warmly before following him to his study, which was situated on the second floor with a magnificent view of the lake and the pope's summer residence at Castel Gandolfo.

'Well, Tom, I don't know what you have got yourself mixed up in, but I assume it's very important and, I would surmise, very dangerous. Cardinal Forcellini, the Vatican Secretary of State, has sent me a letter by personal courier to hand over to you. Also, there is another letter from a student at the Ukrainian College, which was delivered to me by him personally. I have no idea what the letters contain. All I can say is … be careful.'

'Thank you, Monsignor,' said Tom. 'One day I hope I will be able to tell you what this is all about, but for now I have to keep it to myself. I am sure you understand. Would you mind if I read these letters in the privacy of your study?'

'Not at all, Tom. Take as long as you need. I assume you will stay for dinner. And there is a bed for you overnight if you wish.'

'Many thanks. I will take you up on both offers,' Tom said with a grateful smile.

The rector then quietly closed the study door and left Tom to peruse his letters. The one from Joseph Demiuk was not addressed. He opened it and examined six sheets of closely typed lines of letters and numbers. These obviously referred to the book *Three Men in a Boat*, which Bogdan Demiuk had revealed on Yalta beach. He resealed the envelope and put it into his inside pocket, just below his gun holster. Then he opened the other letter delivered by the cardinal's Securicor courier.

It was from Sir Richard Temple. It read,

Tom, after you have read this letter, memorise and destroy its contents. You are to travel to the main Milan railway station the day after you receive this letter, where you will meet another agent on 29 August, who will accompany you back to London. Her name is Lucy McAllinden. She has an Invernessian accent, which I know you are familiar with. She will be dressed in a white miniskirt and a pale blue blouse with a dark blue bead necklace. She will be seated in the station bar at Milan from 5 p.m. until 7 p.m. on the above date.

You will say to her in Italian, 'A nightingale sang in Berkeley Square,' and she will answer in English, 'Yes, but there are golden eagles in the Highlands.' She will have two passports, one for you and one for herself. You will be shown as husband and wife, Mr and Mrs McAllinden. You are both to stay in Milan overnight at the Hotel San Paolo, and catch the Calais express in the morning.

Give Demiuk's letter to Lucy at the hotel. And be very careful. There are indications of Soviet agents moving locations in Europe. It is almost certain that Gudenov is after you.

Good luck.

RT

'Bloody hell,' said Tom. 'Sir Richard is a meticulous planner. I wonder what this Lucy McAllinden is like.' He memorised the message and then destroyed the letter in the rector's shredder, which was conveniently conspicuous behind his desk.

He left the room and went into the garden, where he marvelled at the view over Lago Albano. It brought back many nostalgic memories. He made his way towards the swimming pool through the scented gardens and saw Monsignor Burke sitting on the lower fountain wall with two other people, a man and a woman. Tom walked towards them and was introduced to the couple by the rector.

'Hello again. Tom, may I introduce to you two of our guests who have been staying here for a few days? This is Father Damian Smith and his sister, Julie. Damian is the parish priest of St Peter's in Leicester, but he also has a part-time post as lecturer in philosophy and religious studies at Warwick University. Tomorrow they are driving to Milan to attend a theological course on science, natural law and Church teaching at Milan University. I think he left the English College here a year or two before you arrived. Julie is a teacher in her local school in Nottingham.'

'Well, that's a lucky coincidence,' said Tom. 'I'm due to catch the train for Milan tomorrow.'

'Then why not travel with us in the car instead?' said Father Damian. 'There'll be plenty of room. We're travelling light and I presume you are, so extra luggage wouldn't be a problem.'

'That would be great,' said Tom enthusiastically, 'I only have a small backpack and I would welcome your company for the long journey. It's really kind of you to take me.'

'Good. That's settled,' said Father Damian and looked at his sister, who nodded and smiled.

'It will be a pleasure to have you with us,' said Julie, who had mentally noted Tom's appearance and attractiveness. Even a married devout Catholic woman cannot always resist the temptation to think what she may like to happen, even if it never does.

A bell sounded to give notice that dinner was ready so Monsignor Burke ushered his guests into the refectory, which had started to fill up with students. The three visitors were seated with the rector on the top table.

Before the food was served, grace was said in Latin by the head student. Although the vernacular was now approved for all prayers, some habits were hard to give up. The meal comprised a shrimp antipasto, herb-roasted chicken with a side salad, fresh fruit salad and local cheeses. An excellent wine from nearby Rocca di Papa complemented the meal.

Once dinner was finished, coffee was served on the terrace with a digestivo of brandy or Strega. Tom enjoyed an hour or so chatting with the students, a number of who had been with him when he had spent time at the college several years ago.

However, after a while he began to feel tired. So, mindful of the long journey in the morning, he said his farewells and retired to bed.

37

The Journey to Milan

After an early breakfast Father Damian, his sister Julie and Tom said their farewells to Monsignor Burke and set off in the priest's Fiat on their drive to Milan. It was a beautiful sunny day. After about an hour they joined the main autostrada to the north, which was very busy with both home and foreign traffic. This was to be expected, since it was still the holiday season.

They had travelled for thirty kilometres or so when Father Damian said, 'I think we should take a break at the next service station. We have been travelling for about two hours and I need a pee. Also a cool drink would be very welcome.'

'A good idea,' said Tom, who had been dozing in the back seat. 'Don't you agree, Julie?'

She nodded without hesitation. She was not accustomed to the intense heat of the Italian summer sun, and some shade and a cold drink would be refreshing. They turned off the autostrada just south of Spoleto, where the sign to Florence was clearly marked. They protected their faces, arms and legs with high-density sun barrier cream and made their way to a shaded bar that was situated a little way from the crowded car park.

The three travellers each enjoyed a toasted ham and

cheese sandwich with an ice-cold orange drink. They felt refreshed and ready to resume their journey. As they made their way to the car, Tom thought he recognised a blue Citroën parked near to the car park entrance. He could not say for sure where he had seen it – in Rome, Albano or on the road this morning – so he made a note of the registration number. As they began to leave the service station Tom noticed a tall, athletic man in light beige trousers and a loose-fitting white shirt get into the Citroën. On joining the autostrada Tom noticed that the Citroën was only a few cars behind them.

The priest was obviously a careful driver. He stayed in the middle lane doing a steady sixty kilometres per hour, although he could have gone faster without breaking the speed limit.

'Father Damian,' said Tom, 'what is the maximum speed of this Fiat?'

'It can reach 100 kilometres per hour, but I rarely go much faster than sixty to sixty-five. If you wish, I could put my foot down and give you a demonstration,' replied the priest.

'Yes, that would be great,' said Tom. 'I guess I'm so used to driving fast on motorways back home in my Ford. I am very interested to see how this Fiat performs at high speeds on an Italian motorway.' However, Tom was being economical with the truth. He wanted the Fiat to go faster to see whether the blue Citroën behind them would react by increasing its speed to keep up with them.

'OK, Tom,' said Father Damian, 'let's give it a go. The traffic has eased off a little, and so far I have not seen any police motorway patrols. I'll take the speed up to ninety kilometres per hour, but keep a close watch out of the back window for any police vehicles. I do not wish to create a scandal for speeding. Just imagine the headlines: *Dangerous speeding priest endangers lives.*'

The Fiat responded to the increased acceleration and was soon cruising at ninety kilometres per hour.

Tom looked out of the rear window and saw no police but noticed the Citroën moving into the fast lane from its previous position in the middle lane. The Citroën was obviously keeping the Fiat in its sight but still keeping a few cars' distance away. 'Just as I thought,' Tom said to himself. 'We are being followed.'

Neither Father Damian nor his sister had any idea of his mission. Besides, it could put them in danger if they knew. It was far better that they remained ignorant of what was now becoming a dangerous and life-threatening assignment.

'Well, what do you think, Tom?' asked the priest, as he reduced the speed to sixty-five kilometres per hour and positioned the Fiat once again in the middle lane.

'I'm very impressed. It holds the road well, with no undue shaking, and soon reaches its cruising speed,' said Tom. He also noticed in the side mirror that the blue Citroën had also reduced speed and taken up a position in the middle lane about 100 metres behind them.

The signs for Florence were becoming more frequent when Julie, who had been quiet for most of the journey, asked Tom whether he had ever been to Florence.

'I passed through the city at night about two years ago when a friend and I drove to Rome and back in my old banger – which, I am pleased to say, performed remarkably well. However, we did not have time to stay there and visit its many beautiful churches, monuments and art galleries. I would love to have seen the Renaissance buildings and architecture of the Medici and, of course, the Uffizi. But we had to get back to work and unfortunately ran out of time,' said Tom.

Julie then spoke to her brother. 'Do you think we could stay overnight in Florence? Tom has never seen it in daylight. I am sure we would be made welcome at the convent where we stayed two years ago. And your conference in Milan does not start for another three days.'

'Well, I see no reason why not, if Tom and the nuns agree. What do you think, Tom?' asked Father Damian.

'Suits me fine,' said Tom. 'We could spend most of this late afternoon and evening sightseeing, and visit the Uffizi Gallery tomorrow morning before continuing our journey to Milan.' But, just as importantly for Tom, it would provide an opportunity to lose the blue Citroën in the busy Florentine traffic.

'Good. Then that's settled. We shall have a brief stop at the next service station and telephone the convent.'

'I'll do the telephoning,' said Julie. 'My Italian pronunciation is better than yours, Damian, and a female voice can be reassuring. And we will be generous paying guests.'

The call was made and the bookings agreed. Florence was an hour or so away and it was only 3.30 p.m. Hoping to gain a little more time, Father Damian pressed down on the accelerator, went into the third lane and overtook several cars in the middle lane at seventy-five kilometres per hour. He was beginning to enjoy his new-found pleasure as a racing driver. Both Julie and Tom approved, but it was doubtful whether the driver of the blue Citroën, whom Tom had realised by now was trying to keep them in his sights, shared their enthusiasm.

Their stay in Florence was very enjoyable, particularly the visit to the Uffizi, with its marvellous collection of Renaissance art. It is amazing to consider just how many great painters that period in Italian history produced.

The accommodation at the convent was excellent. After a tasty continental breakfast of cheeses, ham and home-made jam from fruit grown in the large convent garden, the three travellers thanked their attentive hosts and set off through northern Florence to the autostrada. There was still a long drive to Milan but again it was another glorious sunny day. Sensibly, they took several bottles of water with them.

Tom also felt greatly relieved, since the blue Citroën was nowhere to be seen. 'That's good,' he said to himself. 'We must have lost him in the Florentine traffic.'

38

Arrival in Milan

As they approached Milan, Father Damian asked Tom whether he wanted to go to his hotel first or to the railway station. 'The railway station, please,' said Tom. 'I need to find out the train times to Calais and the sleeper arrangements for tomorrow evening.'

'Fine,' said Father Damian, who was able to pick up the road signs for the station as they entered the outskirts of the city. Within half an hour Tom had been dropped off at the station and had said his farewells to Father Damian and Julie.

'Many thanks for the lift. It was kind of you to take me, and it was good to have your company on such a long journey,' said Tom, with a grateful smile and shaking each of their hands in turn. He also gave Julie a kiss on the cheek.

'It was a pleasure having you with us,' Father Damian replied. 'Perhaps we may meet up again sometime. Have a safe journey home and all the very best.' Both brother and sister waved and smiled as they drove off to find their own accommodation at the convent of the Sisters of Mercy. Julie blew a kiss and felt somewhat deflated that Tom was no longer with them.

Tom made his way to the station's lounge bar, mindful of Sir Richard Temple's description of Lucy McAllinden,

He scanned the large lounge, which was bustling with travellers eager to get a snack and a drink before their train departures. At first he could see nobody resembling his female contact. Then, in a corner seat near a cigarette machine next to a window that was slightly ajar, he saw a girl with curly black hair to the nape of her neck, a light blue blouse, a white miniskirt and a necklace of dark blue beads. She was stunning.

That's got to be her, thought Tom.

As he approached her she looked up at him with clear blue eyes. Tom said in perfect Italian, 'Buongiorno, signorina. A nightingale sang in Berkeley Square.'

On hearing this she gave a broad smile and replied in a lovely lilting Inverness accent, 'But we have golden eagles in the Highlands.'

Tom sat down next to her. Both were relieved to have successfully made the rendezvous and both were now wondering how the chemistry between them would work.

'Would you like another coffee?' Tom asked.

'No, thank you. On such a hot day I'd prefer an ice-cold Coca-Cola.'

'Fine. I think I'll have a beer.'

Tom soon returned from the bar with the drinks, which they both sipped in silence. After a few minutes Lucy then said, 'I believe you have something for me.'

'Ah, yes, an important letter. Let's get to the privacy of the hotel and I'll hand it to you there. It's too public here. Also, the letter is at the bottom of my backpack and the handover would be seen by any enemy agent who may be spying on us.'

'Do you think we are being watched?' asked Lucy with

a frown.

'Who knows?' said Tom. 'The bastards could be anywhere. Sir Richard was sure that I had been spotted and warned me in a letter he sent to the Austrian Embassy. He advised a low profile and caution. Come on, let's get a taxi to the hotel.'

They left the cafe lounge bar and headed for the taxi rank. They did not see Giacomo next to the newspaper stand with his head hidden in a newspaper.

Back in Florence, he had followed Father Damian's car to the convent and had seen them take out their hand luggage from their vehicle. Since they were obviously staying the night at the convent, he went to a nearby car sales garage and traded in his blue Citroën for a small white Fiat, one that was identical to thousands of similar cars on Italian roads.

Giacomo then went back to the convent in his new car, noted the Fiat was still in the small convent car park and then booked into a nearby cheap hotel. As an experienced operator he knew not to underestimate the enemy. It would be possible that his previous car had been noted by one or all of the three travellers. His new white Fiat would attract no suspicion.

In Milan Station he saw Tom meet up with Lucy. There was no way he was going to lose them now. He overheard Tom say to the taxi driver, 'Hotel San Paolo, per favore.' Giacomo was familiar with this hotel from a previous assignment about three years ago. He watched the taxi move into the evening traffic before returning to the station car park and his white Fiat.

'Do you know anything about this hotel?' asked Lucy. 'I was given the basic details in my briefing before I left London.'

'Several years ago, on my way back to London, I stayed there overnight. However, I can't remember much about it, except that it was clean, comfortable and I had a decent breakfast.'

The taxi arrived at the hotel within twenty minutes. At reception they booked in as Mr and Mrs McAllinden, showed their passports, which Lucy had brought with her, and picked up their room key, Number 69. Dinner was scheduled between 6.30 p.m. and 9.30 p.m., with the same times in the morning for breakfast.

The room was on the third floor with a magnificent view of the city. It was very spacious, with two easy chairs, a king-size bed, a large dresser, fitted wardrobes and an adjacent bathroom. Telephones were on cabinets either side of the bed and there was a bottle of Prosecco and two tall glasses on the dresser.

'This looks very nice. Sir Richard has certainly not stinted on the cost. What do you think, Mrs McAllinden?' said Tom with a twinkle in his eye.

'Excellent,' said Lucy. 'Let's open the Prosecco, relax for a while and then order dinner.'

'Sounds good to me,' said Tom. He opened the wine, poured Lucy a generous glass and then rang reception for a menu. The menu was brought up to their room. It was extensive and expensive, but Lucy had been given plenty of money for expenses. However, neither were particularly hungry, so they passed on starters and went straight to the main courses. Lucy chose fish and Tom went for chicken, each with a side of salad. For dessert both chose zabaglione with a scoop of ice cream. The Prosecco relaxed them and lightened their mood after a tiring day.

'As a married couple,' said Tom with a smile, 'we'll need to act the part like young marrieds, staring into one another's eyes and so on... You know the sort of thing. Perhaps we ought to consummate our relationship.'

Lucy laughed. 'You may be very attractive, but that's not part of the deal. I hardly know you. But full marks for trying. I'll have to think about it.'

'Well, I hardly know you either, but I'm willing to take a chance with a beautiful girl, with beautiful eyes in a beautiful country.'

Lucy smiled but said nothing and returned to her salad. They lingered over the dessert and finished the Prosecco.

The time was approaching 10 p.m. Lucy stifled a yawn, got up from her chair and made her way to the en suite bathroom. 'I'm sure that as an English gentleman you'll let me have the bed. By pushing the two easy chairs together you will have a very comfortable makeshift bed to sleep on,' she said, smiling sweetly.

'OK, I get it. It's been a long day, you're tired and you need to rest. I'll make do with the chairs, but perhaps another time...?' Tom said, with obvious disappointment in his voice.

'Perhaps, and perhaps not,' she answered, and went into the bathroom.

After about ten minutes she came out and walked towards the bed then turned to face Tom. She was completely naked. Tom just stared at her. He couldn't speak.

'Well, what are you waiting for?'

He needed no more encouragement.

39

A Train Journey With a Difference

Tom woke at 7.45 a.m., but Lucy was still fast asleep. A curly strand of her jet-black hair covered her left eye. He gently stroked it away and gazed at her lovely face as she softly breathed. He could hardly believe the bravery of this young woman on such a dangerous mission.

She soon awoke, smiled at him and said, 'That was so enjoyable. I've had a superb sleep and feel so much better.'

'Same here,' said Tom. 'Do you want breakfast? Would you like a coffee? I could ring down to reception.'

'That sounds good, but we don't have to get up yet. Our train doesn't leave till 8.30 this evening. I'm sure we can think of something to pass the time.' She snuggled up close to him and kissed him full on the lips. They found something to pass the time before coffee and a late breakfast.

They checked out of the hotel at noon and decided to do some sightseeing in this famous northern city, renowned for fashion, football and art. Tom wanted to see the San Siro Stadium but Lucy was interested in the smart shopping streets of the city centre fashion houses. They compromised with an hour at each location before enjoying an evening meal at a well-known trattoria near the magnificent cathedral. They decided to make for the station at 7.30 p.m. By now they were completely at ease with each other. The chemistry between them had worked, as Sir Richard had expected it to.

Giacomo had seen the couple leave the hotel and had tracked them all day as they travelled around the city. He was confident that he had not been seen and followed them back to the station, where he had parked his Fiat down a side street away from the official car park. He saw them having a drink in the station cafe and then walk to Platform 3, where the overnight sleeper to Calais was situated.

He checked his gun. It was secure in its shoulder holster. And the knife was in its sheath.

The sleeper carriages were to the rear of the train. The couple had no difficulty in finding their reservation and decided to make themselves comfortable in the half hour prior to departure. The compartment had two bunk beds and two fixed seats opposite, with a small corner sink.

'Not exactly the Ritz,' said Tom, 'but it should be satisfactory for one night. Which bunk do you want, Lucy, top or bottom?'

'Bottom for me,' said Lucy. 'I'm no good with heights.'

'Ah … a comedian as well as a spy and a femme fatale.' They both laughed, then sat down in the seats to sip their coffee, which they had purchased in the station cafe.

The train pulled out of the station exactly on time and made its way past the cramped high-rise flats, heavy industrial units and row upon row of warehouses that dominated the north of the city.

'How about a meal before we settle down?' suggested Lucy. 'I'm feeling a bit peckish.'

'Good idea,' said Tom. 'I noticed that the restaurant car

was attached to these sleepers, so we won't have far to go.'

The train was now starting to pick up speed. They locked the compartment and Lucy took her handbag, which contained Demiuk's letter.

'Best keep it near and safe,' she said. Tom nodded.

They swayed pleasantly with the train as they made their way to the restaurant car, occasionally stopping when Lucy lost her balance, sometimes deliberately, so she could be caught by Tom, who would kiss the nape of her neck.

There were not many travellers at the tables, and they were able to sit in a window seat about halfway down the carriage. They each chose a pasta dish. Lucy had carbonara and Tom lasagne, with a carafe of Valpolicella wine between them.

The previous day Giacomo had followed the couple back to the hotel and had booked himself a single room for the night. Neither of his prey had seen him, so he was confident that he would not be recognised. However, to be on the safe side, he had left his car in the station car park and taken a taxi to the hotel, asking the driver to follow the one that Tom and Lucy were being driven in.

He decided not to go down to the hotel's restaurant but asked room service to bring him up a pizza and a beer. In the morning he had followed the couple back to the station and booked himself on their train but only with a seat reservation to Paris. He would get done what he needed to long before arrival in the French capital. There was no need for a sleeper. He had kept watch on the movements of the couple during the day, had seen them board the train and had decided to do the same. He noted their sleeper compartment number and then settled down to read his paper and wait.

After their evening meal Lucy and Tom returned to their compartment and decided to settle down for the night.

'I just need to visit the toilet at the end of the corridor and freshen up a bit. I shan't be long,' Lucy said as she opened the sliding door.

Tom sat down to check over the train route as Lucy left the compartment. She was only gone for a short time when the door slid open again. Tom did not look up but commented in a rather surprised voice, 'Well, you didn't take very long. Did you miss me?' he asked jokingly.

'Good evening, Mr Bond,' said a mocking, heavily accented English voice. 'We meet, at last.'

Tom looked up in amazement to see Giacomo with a knife at Lucy's throat. The door was closed with a metallic clang.

'Take out your gun slowly – I know you must have one – and throw it onto the bunk bed, or else your pretty so-called wife will not look so pretty.'

Tom did as he was told.

'Now, both hands above your head and stand by the window.'

Lucy's face was drained of colour and her frightened eyes were fixed on Tom. A thin trickle of blood ran down her neck and between her breasts, the result of a small cut of Giacomo's knife. The Italian needed to show Tom that he meant what he said.

'I believe you have something for me,' he said with a wide grin. 'A letter from Signor Demiuk?'

'I do not have any letter,' Tom said truthfully in perfect Italian.

'Do not lie to me, Mr Bond, or this sharp knife may disfigure your girlfriend's throat.'

Lucy's arms were pinned across her chest by Giacomo's left hand and arm, but she was able to slightly raise her hand.

'He's telling the truth,' she said in a gasp. 'I have the letter.'

'Where?'

'In my handbag, on the top bunk.'

'Get it down and give it to me,' Giacomo said in a growl, as he twisted her towards the bunks, the knife still at her throat. 'But first bend down and give me the gun.'

She obeyed her captor and retrieved her handbag.

'Take the letter out and give it to me. I will release your hands to get it but will keep the knife on your pretty neck. So no tricks.'

Lucy saw the letter folded longways in her bag next to her tail comb. Giacomo's eyes were trained on Tom, with an occasional glance at Lucy's hands. She deftly hid the tail comb in the folds of the letter and held it up for Giacomo to reach.

'Thank you, signorina. It is so sad that you and your friend have to die,' said the killer. But, as he went to take the letter, Lucy felt the blade of the knife briefly come off her skin.

With all her might, in a backward swing, she stabbed the metal handle of the tail comb into Giacomo's stomach. He cried out with pain and the knife dropped to the floor. He sagged to his knees and Tom, seeing his chance, kicked him with full force in the face.

Tom grabbed his gun and was about to shoot the Italian

when Lucy shouted, 'No. He will be dead in a few minutes.'

'What do you mean? He will be only stunned. We should finish him off before he does for us,' said a frantic Tom.

'The metallic handle of the tail comb contained a deadly poison. He will not survive.'

40

Goodbye Giacomo

Giacomo's breathing became laboured, then intermittent. Then there was silence. Suddenly he coughed blood out of his mouth and down his white shirt. He was not a pretty sight.

'So what do we do now? This sort of thing isn't in my job description,' said an anguished Tom.

'First we stop his bleeding. Stuff your paper into his mouth. Then go to the toilet at the end of this corridor to get some plasters from the complimentary first aid kit to patch up his stomach wound.'

Lucy then began to wipe up the blood on the floor of the compartment with paper tissues and handkerchiefs from her handbag. Tom soon returned with the plasters, a large toilet roll and another towel. He patched up Giacomo's stomach and helped Lucy to mop up the blood.

'We need to clean up, so as not to give the train attendants any immediate suspicion. We also need to dispose of his body. Any ideas?' she asked.

'In about two hours we cross the Rhône. If we get him to the door at the end of carriage, near the toilet, we can heave him out into the river below.'

'Good thinking,' said Lucy, her hands stained with blood. 'Put one of those plasters on the cut on my throat.

It seems to have stopped bleeding now. Another quarter inch and the bastard would have killed me. I'm going to the toilet to wash and change my clothes.'

When she returned, Tom had already propped Giacomo's body against the bottom bunk, but his head lolled onto the mattress.

'What a bloody awful job this is,' said Tom. 'How did you get involved with such gruesome killings?'

'It's a long story. Not for now. It's not always like this, but you can never underestimate or foresee the risk of an assignment.'

He shrugged in disbelief. 'We need to wait for an hour or so before we reach the Rhône. I think a stiff drink is called for, and a ciggie. I don't know about you, but it will settle my nerves.'

'Agreed,' said Lucy. 'We should celebrate that we're still alive.'

After half an hour the couple returned to their compartment. Fortunately, there were only two other sleeper compartments taken in their carriage, and no sound could be heard from either of them.

'We shall be at the bridge in about twenty minutes. Better get the body to the end of the corridor,' said Tom.

'Right,' said Lucy. 'You get his top half and I'll lift his legs. Nobody seems to be stirring in the other compartments.'

Tom put his arms under Giacomo's shoulders and dragged him along the corridor floor. Lucy helped by lifting his feet, but he was too heavy to lift both his legs.

'What a bloody weight,' said Tom, gasping.

They had to manoeuvre the body in stages, but they eventually reached the end of the corridor and sat Giacomo up against the outer door.

It was then that they heard another compartment door open and footsteps coming down the corridor. Obviously it was another sleeper passenger needing to use the toilet.

'Oh, shit,' muttered Tom. But Lucy made a drinking sign and pointed to the body and figuratively rolled her head. Tom understood and nodded.

As the passenger came to the end of the corridor and saw Giacomo and the couple kneeling beside him, he asked in complete surprise,

'What's the matter with him? Is he ill?'

'No. I'm afraid he is very drunk, but we are friends and will help him,' said Tom.

The passenger nodded and entered the toilet cubicle. As he came out, he wished the couple good luck and returned to his compartment.

'That was a close shave,' said Tom. 'We need to stand the bastard up ready for his departure. I can clearly see the bridge now. Get ready, Lucy, to open the door when I say so.'

The train sped onto the bridge. Tom held Giacomo's body against the carriage door.

'Now,' he yelled, through the siren sounds of the hooting train and the metallic sounds of the wheels on the rails. As the door swung open Tom pushed the body with all his strength and saw it bounce over the side rails of the bridge and into the grey waters below.

'Good riddance,' Tom exclaimed, and after grabbing the swinging carriage door he firmly shut it.

'Job done. We now need some rest before we reach the ferry,' said an exhausted Lucy. Her strained faced said it all.

The couple returned to their compartment and lay on their bunks, thankful for some fitful sleep before arriving in Calais. When they arrived there they quickly disembarked from the train and secured good seats on the ferry. They slept and dozed most of the sea journey to Dover. The drama and exertions of the night had left them drained.

On arrival at the English port they made their way to the railway station and caught the first available train to London. They arrived in the capital in the middle of the afternoon and took a taxi to MI6 headquarters, where they were seen immediately by Sir Richard Temple. Another colleague joined the MI6 head and a thorough debriefing took place.

'You have both done exceptionally well,' said Sir Richard. 'But first, do you have the name of the book used by Demiuk and his accompanying letter?'

Tom confirmed the book as *Three Men in a Boat* by Jerome K. Jerome, the first edition, and Lucy took out the letter from her handbag and gave it to her boss.

'Don't worry about the disposal of your assailant. I will speak with the French authorities, who will clear up any problems which may occur. You both look completely shattered. As a small reward, I have booked you a couple of days in the Ritz. So relax and enjoy yourselves.' He smiled and gave them a knowing wink.

'Thank you, sir,' said Tom. 'Do you have any news of my friends?'

'No, but as soon as I do I will contact you immediately.'

They shook hands and agreed to meet in two days' time. The couple then left for the Ritz.

41

From Vienna to Calais

Having said their goodbyes to Tom at Vienna Station, Dunk and Bernie returned to the car and began the journey to Calais and the ferry to Dover. Dunk took the wheel for the first leg of the journey through northern Austria and into West Germany, and then headed towards the Dutch border.

Dunk examined the gun that they had picked up at the embassy. It was a Luger automatic. His experience with guns and his mechanical brain soon understood how it worked, and he examined the main parts: the barrel, the bullet magazine and the trigger function. He showed Bernie, who listened intently to his friend's explanations, how to use the gun. Dunk said that he was familiar with that model from his knowledge acquired from his days in the Highland Gun Club.

'When we swap round in an hour or so, I'll give you a demonstration of how to fire it,' said Dunk. 'There's nothing to it so long as it's loaded. The bullets are inside, and you squeeze the trigger rather than snatch at it.'

'OK, M,' said Bernie. 'You're the expert.'

Heinrich Mueller had not expected the friends to separate in Vienna, and now he needed two more agents to follow Dunk and Bernie, since Hans Lassis and Kurt Neuerbach had been tailing Tom on the train to Rome. He telephoned Bertrand Schlesinger and Otto Bosch, who were both competent and ruthless agents. He explained to them why Gudenov wanted Bernie and Dunk eliminated, and that on completion of their assignment a generous bonus would be paid by the Soviet authorities.

Mueller described the physical appearance of their intended victims and the make, colour and registration number of the car they were driving. He also outlined the proposed route of the British tourists, who were no doubt heading for one of the Channel ports. Mueller then telephoned Gudenov, who was effusive in his praise for the German spymaster's initiative.

Schlesinger and Bosch did not expect to see many old dirty-white UK-registered cars on the road, and it was not long before they spotted their quarry. They kept about 100 metres behind the old Ford. They were driving a silver VW and were utterly inconspicuous, like hundreds of other vehicles travelling the motorways.

'This job should be fairly easy,' said Bertrand. 'In about fifty kilometres the road will skirt the mountainside – which, as you know, Otto, has a very steep drop on the driver's side. We will come up behind them and ram their car hard, to send it hurtling through the barrier and down onto the rocks below. No one would be able to survive such a crash.'

'An excellent plan, my friend. We could then motor into Bavaria and celebrate our success with some first-rate beer and schnapps.'

Dunk and Bernie pulled into a service station, had a pee, grabbed a coffee and then returned to the car. They drove to a quiet part of the open forecourt behind the payment point and shop where no one could see them. Dunk then demonstrated to Bernie how to use the gun.

'Hopefully we won't have to use it, but it's as well that both of us know how to handle it if we have to,' said Dunk.

Dunk, now in the driver's seat, started up the engine and rejoined the motorway.

The road began to rise as the mountain came into view. The scenery was spectacular. There was cultivated, rolling farmland on the lowland plains and wooded foothills on the lower slopes, which then stopped abruptly at the barren rock face of the mountain.

The two friends admired the view and decided to pull into a convenient lay-by to take photographs. They noticed that another car, some way behind them, had also stopped. A man got out and seemed to be using binoculars. He appeared to be scanning the scenery but also noting the position of Dunk and Bernie. It was Bertrand.

'I remember seeing that VW on the lower motorway,' said Dunk. 'We need to be suspicious and careful.'

Bernie agreed as they rejoined the narrowing road as it wound up the mountainside. After about twenty minutes the road reached a plateau, where it remained straight and flat for about half a kilometre. There was no oncoming traffic, the sun was hot and there was no cooling breeze. Suddenly Dunk noticed in the rear-view mirror that the silver VW had picked up speed and was approaching fast. There were no signs or indicators that the vehicle intended to overtake.

'Bernie, we have a problem. Get the gun ready in case we need it.'

'Right. I have it in my hand, finger on the trigger.'

Bernie turned round to see the VW within a few metres, tailgating the Ford. Then there was a mighty bang on the rear bumper. A shot was aimed at Bernie's head by Otto, which parted his hair and blew away his sun hat.

'You bastard,' yelled Bernie, who leant over the car door and fired a retaliatory shot, which shattered the VW's windscreen.

Dunk immediately pulled over onto the right side of the road and did an emergency stop. The VW suddenly overtook them in the left-hand lane as Bertrand grappled with the steering and tried to keep the car under control, since the cracked windscreen had drastically reduced his vision.

Dunk saw his advantage and drove hard into the side of the Germans' car. Bernie took aim again and the bullet penetrated Otto's left temple. He fell sideways onto Bertrand's right arm and wrist, causing his companion to swerve and scrape the roadside barrier.

Blood started to pump out of Otto's head onto the driver's hands. The VW was still holding the road. However, the straight stretch was nearing its end. Ahead there was a sharp hairpin bend as the road swung round to the left of the mountainside.

'Shoot the bloody driver,' shouted Dunk, 'before he recovers control. Or else the bastard will come after us again. This old Ford is no match for their VW.'

Bernie took aim and shot the German in the lower neck. There was a sudden grinding noise as the VW hit the roadside barrier and then started to increase its speed. Bertrand's foot had pressed on the accelerator and became trapped, which caused high fuel injection and increased speed. The car had now reached eighty kilometres and was heading directly towards the road barrier on the approaching corner.

The crash was spectacular. The VW was lifted several feet into the air before bouncing down the rocky mountainside to the woods below. Dunk and Bernie drove into a passing place on the corner just in time to see the VW explode in a ball of fire.

They both stood there, shaken but relieved. 'That was supposed to be us,' said Dunk in a whisper. 'Those bastards were sent to kill us.'

By now a couple of cars had also stopped to gawp at the burning car.

'Come on,' said Bernie. 'We need to bugger off now before the cops arrive and start asking questions.'

Within minutes they had resumed their journey, in silence. Neither felt like speaking.

They drove fast to Calais and caught the next available ferry to Dover. They were now more relaxed but still did not speak much. Exhaustion and the fateful outcome of what was supposed to be a safe but adventurous holiday weighed heavily upon them.

When they arrived in Dover it was beginning to get dark, so they decided to pitch the tent in a field just outside the town. They awoke early, brewed a mug of tea and then set off for London.

They met Sir Richard at around 2 p.m. that afternoon. Just as he had done with Tom and Lucy the day before, the MI6 chief thoroughly debriefed the two friends. The minutest details were gone over meticulously, particularly their time in Yalta and Vienna, and the journey to Calais, with the killing of the two German agents.

'Very well done to all of you. I am sure the Americans will be effusive with their praise and congratulations. Your friend Tom was anxious to hear news of you. Why not give him a surprise? He's relaxing at the Ritz. I am sure he will be delighted to see you both. I've also booked rooms for you there as well for a little R & R. However, I want to see all four of you in a couple of days' time along with your head of department,' said Sir Richard.

'Thank you, sir,' said Bernie.

'Did you say all *four* of us?' queried Dunk.

'Yes. One of my agents is with your friend. Tom needed some expert help, so I supplied it. No doubt he will explain all when you see him.'

42

Back in London

Dunk and Bernie made their way to the Ritz and asked at reception for a Mr Tom Gillespie. They were very surprised when they were told that no one of that name was staying at the hotel.

'Let's check the bar. If he is going to be anywhere at this time of day, it will be there,' said Dunk.

Sure enough, Tom was there in a plush easy chair enjoying his favourite dram, an eighteen-year-old Macallan. Next to him sat Lucy, looking beautiful in a pink blouse, a pink miniskirt, pink dress shoes and a white flower in her gorgeous black curly hair.

'He doesn't waste any time getting a bird,' said Bernie, with a broad smile. 'Well, well, fancy seeing you here with this gorgeous creature. Are you going to introduce us?'

'This is Lucy McAllinden,' said Tom with a big smile. 'She works for MI6 and is my official wife. I'll fill you in with all the details. But it's great to see you two again safe and well.'

The three friends shook hands and embraced one another. Dunk and Bernie went over to Lucy and gave her a kiss and a hug. They then relayed everything that had transpired since they had split up in Vienna. The drink flowed, along with laughter and astonishment at their dangerous escapades.

Two days later they went to MI6 headquarters, where they were met by Sir Richard Temple himself. He took them down a long corridor to an imposing oak-panelled door that opened into a spacious room. Two men and a woman sat in comfortable wine-red armchairs. All three stood up to meet the four young people, and Sir Richard did the introductions.

'This is David Tompkins, our Foreign Secretary. I am sure you will have seen him on TV or in the newspapers. And this is Mr Strobe Delaney, the American ambassador. Of course you three will know your boss, Veronica Johnson, but I don't think Lucy has had the pleasure.'

The Foreign Secretary thanked them on behalf of the prime minister, Harold Wilson, and the government for the success of their mission. The ambassador did likewise, with a special message from President Johnson. As vice president to President Kennedy in 1961 he had been in charge of NASA when the president had made his ambitious speech on 25 May that year.

As chairwoman of HM Customs and Excise, Veronica Johnson endorsed the comments of the Foreign Secretary and the ambassador and added how relieved she was that they had returned safely.

'I think you have had enough danger and adventure to last a lifetime. It's time you returned to a less stressful and more predictable way of living. You will be allowed another week's holiday to see your families, and then it's back to work.'

Mrs Johnson had a gift for bringing people back to earth. Before they left the room Sir Richard said he had an important proposition to make.

'Since you acquitted yourselves so well on a very complex mission, I am offering all three of you the opportunity to join MI6. As you are aware, it is dangerous but challenging work. You would receive intense training both here and abroad, and your salaries would increase substantially. I don't expect a decision from you today. Discuss it among yourselves and let me know when you finally decide.'

'And,' interjected the Foreign Secretary, 'you will each receive two thousand pounds as a reward for your successful assignment.'

The friends thanked their distinguished superiors, shook hands with them and left the building to return to the Ritz. They had one final night left in London before going off to see their families and then back to work.

'Let's have our last night here in Soho,' said Tom. 'We know some good pubs there from our days at the Customs and Excise training centre and when we worked in the Central London region.'

Bernie and Dunk enthusiastically agreed.

'What about you, Lucy? Do you fancy joining us? asked Dunk.

'Oh, yes, that would be great. And I can recommend a superb Italian restaurant in Soho, called La Colombina d'Oro, not far from the Raymond Revuebar, which I'm sure you three know very well.'

'Right. Well, that's settled,' said Bernie. 'Let's meet in the bar at 6.30 p.m. for a quick one, then we'll be off to paint the town red.'

The four of them had a marvellous time, finishing in the Italian trattoria suggested by Lucy. They had spoken at some length about Sir Richard's proposal, but no decisions were made.

On their return to the hotel, a little the worse for wear, they settled for a nightcap and ignored the amused grin of the bartender and his pithy remark. 'You're as pissed as farts,' he said.

The next morning, after a long lie-in and plenty of glasses of water, they met in the restaurant for a full English breakfast – or, in the case of Lucy and Dunk, a full Scottish.

'Well, it's time to get on the M1 to Chesterfield, so that Dunk can pick up his car and you can see your parents, Tom,' said Bernie. 'What are your plans, Lucy?'

'I shall get tonight's sleeper to Inverness, but I need to pick up a few things from my flat first.' She gave Tom a questioning look.

'You two wait for me in the foyer. I need to have a private word with Lucy,' said Tom, picking up the hint.

Dunk and Bernie winked at each other. 'Sure. See you soon in the foyer.'

It was Lucy who spoke first. 'We've been through a lot together in such a short time. We have made love several times. Both of us have enjoyed that enormously. We have got to know each other, our pasts, the present, our work and some details of our families. We also killed a man and threw his body into a river. So do you want to see me again? Do we have a future?'

She held his gaze without revealing her emotions, which were churning around inside her like a combine harvester.

Tom smiled and said, 'Yes, I'd love to see you again, but on one condition: that you do not bring your tail comb within a hundred metres of me.'

She laughed out loud. 'Agreed,' she said, feeling immensely relieved and excited. She would have to finish with her present boyfriend, Dave, but she would do it as gently as she could, since he was a nice chap. But he could not compare to Tom.

It was a month before they met again, but they had kept in touch by telephone and regular letters. Tom had also considered Sir Richard's offer to join MI6 and had decided to take it up. He was fully aware of the risks, but because he would be based in London he could also be with Lucy.

Naturally she was delighted at his decision. They got engaged within six months and married in the spring of 1969.

Epilogue

Dunk and Bernie decided to remain with HM Customs and Excise. Both were eventually promoted to senior positions in the service and enjoyed successful careers.

Within three years at MI6, Tom had had assignments in Poland, East Germany and Hungary. He was then sent to the Ukraine. There an espionage plan went horribly wrong, resulting in him being shot and severely wounded in the chest and neck. He survived death by the prompt action of his colleague, who was able to get him to a local hospital, where he received the immediate attention that saved his life. The British Embassy then flew him back to London to continue further treatment.

Fortunately he made a full recovery, but decided that a less stressful life was what he needed. He resigned from MI6 and decided to return to his former department, where he was appointed as an Excise officer in a Highland Distillery just south of Inverness.

Lucy also resigned her position and was delighted to be returning to her home city. The three friends and their wives met up every year throughout their working lives and still continue to do so during their retirement. Obviously, the summer holiday of 1967 is always a major topic of their conversation.

Gudenov was disgraced for failing to protect the vital secrets of the USSR. He was banished to Siberia, where his health failed, and he succumbed to an early death.

Loda married a local Party official, resigned from the KGB and became a schoolteacher in Yalta.

Bogdan Demiuk and his family were granted political asylum in the UK. He changed his name and settled in Edinburgh.

Joseph Demiuk was ordained a priest in the Catholic Ukrainian Church in 1972. However, as Bogdan's brother, he was constantly harassed by the intelligence authorities. He therefore sought political asylum in the UK, which was successful in March 1973. He was welcomed into the Diocese of Westminster, where he was noticed by Cardinal Heenan as a pastor for immigrants and asylum-seekers and given the job of helping such people settle in the UK.

Monsignor Burke was eventually made a bishop, and he returned to England to administer a diocese in the Midlands. He was later appointed to the Vatican's foreign ministry as an archbishop and served as a papal nuncio. He received his red hat as cardinal in the final consistory of Pope Paul VI.

Heinrich Mueller was sacked by the East German Politburo as head of counter-espionage but was retained in a much lower-grade post, owing to his immense knowledge and contacts.

Franco Pasolini remained General Secretary of the Italian Communist Party until his retirement. The disappearance of Giacomo Beronni was a complete mystery to him. There could be only two plausible explanations: either he was dead or else he had decided to start a completely new life in a foreign land. He was unable to decide which option was more likely.

Giacomo Beronni's body was eventually discovered washed up on the lower banks of the Rhône about four miles from the bridge by an elderly dog walker. The man contacted the police but the corpse was grotesquely disfigured, since it had been in the water for several days. The police assumed that the deceased must have been a homeless man who had suffered an accident or a similar misadventure. The police had no record of anybody being reported as missing within a hundred-kilometre radius. The body was treated with respect and cremated, with the local priest officiating at a short service attended by two compassionate parishioners.

The two East German agents, Hans Lassis and Kurt Neuerbach, continued in the security service. They had successfully completed their part in the surveillance operations in Vienna and Rome.

The burnt and mangled bodies of Bertrand Schlessinger and Otto Bosch were repatriated to East Germany and awarded funerals with full military honours, despite the failure of their assignment. For several years prior to their deaths they had given excellent service to the state and its allies. This deserved to be recognised.

Father Damian Smith eventually became the vicar general of his diocese and became a visiting lecturer in moral theology at the Gregorian University in Rome. His sister Julie became the head teacher of her school.

And finally, on 20 July 1969, Neil Armstrong landed on the Moon and said those famous words, 'That's one small step for a man, one giant leap for mankind.' He had fulfilled President John Fitzgerald Kennedy's wish and given the American people and the West a definitive advantage in their bitter rivalry with the Soviet Union.

But very few people knew that the Apollo rocket that took the astronauts to the Moon was only possible because three young British men had risked their lives on a summer holiday.

Acknowledgements

The companionship and suggestions of my two friends, Iain Matheson (Dunk) and Hugh Burnard (Bernie) has been essential in the planning and completion of the book.

Maureen Nitrato-Izzo, my sister, did a full preliminary editing of the draft manuscript, as well as highlighting inconsistencies and acceptability in text and expression.

Patricia Comb, the Chairwoman of the Filey Saturday morning creative writing group, did an edit similar to my sister, particularly examining punctuation and format.

The professional staff of 2QT Publishing edited the final text and cover design to ensure that the book would be print ready. Their advice and cooperation were excellent.

.

Lightning Source UK Ltd.
Milton Keynes UK
UKHW011052060722
405457UK00002B/490